LARRY

When

McMurtry

the Light Goes

A Novel

SIMON & SCHUSTER PAPERBACKS
New York London Toronto Sydney

SIMON & SCHUSTER PAPERBACKS
Rockefeller Center
1230 Avenue of the Americas
New York, NY 10020

First Simon & Schuster trade paperback March 2008

SIMON & SCHUSTER PAPERBACKS and colophon are registered trademarks of Simon & Schuster, Inc.

For information about special discounts for bulk purchases, please contact Simon & Schuster Special Sales at 1-800-456-6798 or business@simonandschuster.com

Designed by Karolina Harris

Manufactured in the United States of America

3   5   7   9   10   8   6   4   2

The Library of Congress has cataloged the hardcover edition as follows:

McMurtry, Larry.

When the light goes : a novel / Larry McMurtry.

p. cm.

Sequel to: Duane's depressed.

1. Older men—Fiction. 2. Thalia (Tex. : Imaginary place)—Fiction. 3. City and town life—Fiction.

4. Texas—Fiction. I. Title.

PS3563.A319W47 2007

813'.54—dc22   2006050821

ISBN-13: 978-1-4165-3426-6
ISBN-10: 1-4165-3426-1
ISBN-13: 978-1-4165-3427-3 (pbk)
ISBN-10: 1-4165-3427-X (pbk)

For James
For Curtis
For Gail

To conquer isolation is the aim of most villages . . .

SMALL-TOWN MAYOR, FRENCH,
QUOTED BY JANET FLANNER IN *PARIS JOURNAL II*

1

"WOW, LOOK AT THOSE TWO!" the young woman exclaimed—by "those two" she seemed to be referring to her own stiffening nipples, plainly visible beneath a pale shirt that showed her small breasts as clearly as if she had been naked.

"Hard as little pickles," she said pleasantly, standing up to shake Duane's hand.

"I'm Annie," she added. "Annie Cameron—and you're Mr. Moore—or I certainly do hope you're Mr. Moore."

Annie Cameron looked alert and smart, wore no makeup, and had her dark hair pulled back in a ponytail.

Duane had just returned from Egypt. He had only that moment stepped into the Thalia office of his small oil company, and he had never seen the young woman with the hard-as-little-pickles nipples before. A dark green Lexus was parked outside the office—a car he had also never seen before.

"See any good belly dancing while you were in Cairo?" Annie asked—probably she realized that Duane was momentarily at a loss for words.

"I didn't get around to the belly dancing," he admitted, wondering how this smart-looking, rangy young woman with the delightful smile had found her way to his old office in Thalia. It had been his *only* office until he had more or less retreated—both from the oil business *and* from family life as he had lived it for forty years—to a cabin on a nearby hill. His elder son, Dickie Moore, now ran the drilling company from a larger and more modern office in Wichita Falls, where the company's masses of equipment—trucks, pickups, pulling machines, drill bits, cables, extra pipe and the like could be housed until needed.

Very little active work got done in the Thalia office, which made the sudden, vivid presence of Anne Cameron even more of a mystery.

Anne Cameron looked Duane directly in the eye for a moment, and then slipped back into her seat behind a new, expensive-looking computer.

"Just let me finish this one graph," she said. "I'm checking some wells Moore Drilling dug in Young County in the early Seventies." She clicked rapidly for a minute or two and then Duane heard the low hum of the printer.

"I find I can't be very social until I'm at a good stopping place in whatever analysis I'm doing," she said. "I'm just too much of a perfectionist—my mother says my perfectionism is why I'm single."

"She may have a point," Duane said.

He felt at something of a loss. Yesterday he had arrived in Brooklyn, on a freighter from Alexandria, Egypt. The freighter was called the *Tappan Zee*. This morning he had flown to Dallas, and then on to Wichita Falls, where, two weeks earlier, he had left his bicycle chained to a sapling in the airport parking lot. On the long bumpy flight to Dallas he had begun to worry about the bicycle, an expensive machine made exactly to his specifications. Yet he had left it vulnerable to anyone with a chain-cutter, and there were plenty of those in the oil patch. They could easily have snipped the chain and taken the bike. His relief, when he saw that his bike was still there, was great. He unchained the bike and rode it through August heat the twenty-two miles to Thalia. Thanks mainly to the fact that his bicycle hadn't been stolen, he was in a fairly upbeat mood. Two of his own trucks passed him as he was pedaling, but neither driver gave him so much as a toot of the horn. They were all well used to seeing the boss on his bicycle—besides, in practical terms, he was no longer their boss: Dickie was their boss.

Duane badly needed a shave and a shower but felt he might as well stop by the office for a minute, to let everyone know that he was back. He expected to find his small Thalia crew at one another's throats—that was their usual condition. Earlene, the much fired, much rehired secretary, would be there, misfiling things. Ruth Popper, edging into her mid-nineties now, would be rocking in her corner, doing crosswords that she was too blind to really see. And Bobby Lee, who had worked for Duane since they were teenagers, would be on the outs with Earlene or Ruth or both.

Instead, when he stepped into the office, he found Anne Cameron and her stiff nipples. Besides the nipples there was also the expensive new computer in an office that had been all but abandoned by the young powers-that-be at Moore Drilling.

Suddenly Anne stopped clicking at her keyboard and looked at Duane with doubt in her expression.

"Is it because of my titties that you're looking that way, Mr. Moore?" she asked. "I hope you're not thinking I'm flirty. Sometimes I let myself daydream about Ruel, which is why my little pickles poked up. Ruel was my sexiest boyfriend ever.

"In fact he was my only sexy boyfriend. Most of the time I dated computer geeks."

Duane could think of no reply.

"I always mean to dress conservatively, but then I don't," she added. "It's my California heritage, I guess. I don't have big boobs, so why wear a bra? What do you think?"

Duane thought that Anne Cameron, nipples or no, was a huge improvement on what he had expected to find when he pedaled up to his office.

He didn't say it, though.

"I've been to Egypt," he reminded her. "I didn't get around to the belly dancing but I did see the pyramids. Now I'm home and I think I need a nap."

Anne Cameron looked relieved, if not entirely convinced.

"Dickie said you'd be mighty surprised when you saw me," she said.

Duane felt tired.

Annie was clicking rapidly when he went out the door.

2

DUANE'S BIG HOUSE on the edge of Thalia—it was the spacious ranch-style home where he and Karla, his wonderful wife of forty years, had raised their four children and most of their nine grandchildren—was only a few blocks from the office where Anne Cameron was busy on the computer. What exactly she was doing on the new, pricey computer Duane could not say.

His wife, Karla, had been killed two years before, in a head-on collision with a milk truck on the curve of a narrow Texas farm-to-market road. She had been on her way to Dallas for a day of shopping—had she survived she would have undoubtedly brought home lots of expensive clothes to stuff in closets already tightly stuffed with expensive clothes.

Duane was on the back steps of his house, attempting to dig his house keys out of the small backpack, which contained his passport, a change of clothes, two changes of underwear, and a small paperback guide to Cairo and its environs, when he realized that he didn't really want to go into his house, where, at the moment, no one lived at all. He wanted a shave and a shower but he didn't want to perform either activity in this big, darkened, silent house.

Ruth Popper, technically still his employee but, untechnically, probably his oldest and closest friend in the town of Thalia, lived only a few blocks away—indeed, in strict truth, everyone in Thalia lived only a few blocks away. It was not a particularly spread-out town. Though Ruth had felt free to criticize Duane's behavior virtually every day for fifty years, he nonetheless felt sure she would allow him the shower and the shave. Then, refreshed, he could bicycle out to his cabin, six miles from town, and watch the long August sunset from the edge of his hill.

Though now nearly blind, Ruth had lived in her small house so long that she could move about it unerringly, or almost. A year before she had stumbled over a footstool that wasn't where it was supposed to be, breaking her left arm in two places but sparing her hips at least.

As usual Ruth blamed Bobby Lee for this setback.

"Bobby Lee was the last person to sit on that footstool, so it's no wonder he left it where it would trip me," she pointed out. Ruth and Bobby were bitter, lifelong rivals for Duane's attention— each would automatically blame the other for any error made in the operation of the drilling company—and, over the decades, thousands of errors had been made by the various employees of Moore Drilling.

"Ten a day, at least, for forty-one years, if somebody would like to put a calculator on it!" Duane said once.

Nobody wanted to put a calculator on it.

When Duane rang her doorbell Ruth began a slow and cautious approach to her front door.

"Hold your horses! Hold your horses!" she said, several times.

"I only rang once," Duane pointed out, when Ruth finally opened the door. "I *did* hold my horses."

"Yes, but you're impatient by nature," Ruth told him. "I guess I know that much about you.

"Were the pyramids worth it?" she asked, when he stepped inside. Ruth had gone to Egypt with her sister Billie—the sisters had also gone to Russia and China and various other places—and had strongly encouraged Duane to start with the pyramids if he ever set out to see the world.

"The pyramids were worth it," Duane assured her. "They were the most worth it of anything I've ever seen in my life—or am ever likely to see. May I use your shower?"

"They don't give away water in this town," Ruth reminded him, sharply. "What's wrong with *your* shower?"

"It's in my house," Duane reminded her. "Going to Egypt was easy, but going into my house is hard."

"Oh, help yourself, Duane," Ruth said. "You could use a shave too while you're at it."

"How do you know I need a shave?" Duane asked. "You can't see well enough to see my stubble."

"It's the way you sound, Duane," Ruth assured him. "You sound all growly when you need a shave."

Duane, never one to waste water, shaved quickly and then took a steaming hot shower and emerged refreshed. He had had his change of clothes laundered on the big ship; he felt perked up and ready for a brisk ride out to his cabin.

"Why can't you go into your own house, Duane?" Ruth asked, as he was at the door.

"It's the pictures on the icebox door," he said. "Mine and Karla's whole life together is on that door. The kids. The grand-kids. Nellie being crowned homecoming queen. Little Bascom showing off his first tooth. Karla . . ."

He had to stop for a bit, at the thought of his late wife.

"Karla and me, getting drunk in Colorado," he said. "Karla and me when we were young and happy."

"And middle-aged and happy?" Ruth asked.

"Middle-aged and struggling, but hell! At least we were still married."

"It's a refrigerator door, Duane—stop calling it an icebox, it dates you," Ruth said. It was an attempt to get Duane's mind off Karla, about whom, she knew, he felt a lot of guilt. After all, if he hadn't parked his pickup and started walking everywhere, and then had gone so far as to move out to his cabin, Karla might not have been speeding eastbound just as the milk truck came speeding westbound, into the same curve.

Duane caught himself just in time. He backed away from the subject of Karla and their happiness or unhappiness, as traced by the many family pictures stuck on the icebox door.

"By the way, Ruth," he asked, "who's this Anne Cameron who seems to be running the Thalia office now?"

"She's not running the office," Ruth said. "She's a geological analyst—she went to MIT and Caltech too. Unless I miss my guess she's also your next wife."

"That girl? No way," Duane said. "She's younger than my daughters—way younger."

"So what?" Ruth came back. "Most men at your age marry women who are younger than their daughters. It's perfectly normal."

"Even if it is, what if I don't want a next wife?" Duane asked, a little too loudly.

"No, you'd rather take showers at my house than face the fact, which is that Karla is dead and your children are grown up and gone. Your grandkids are gone too, and they're also nearly grown up. You're a family man with an empty nest. What you need to do is start a new family with a smart young geological analyst with a couple of good degrees.

"And you don't need to bark at me, either," Ruth reminded him.

"I'm sorry," he said. He often barked at Ruth and then apologized for his rudeness. She had, after all, been one of his most maddening employees for over forty years.

"It's all right, honey," Ruth said. Sometimes she called Duane honey and sometimes he called her honey, in acknowledgment of the fact that they had meant a lot to one another for a long time—for most of their lives, in fact.

"I bet you're just jet-lagged," Ruth ventured. "When my sister and I flew home from Russia I was jet-lagged for a whole month. Nobody could put up with me."

"I'm not jet-lagged—I came home on a ship, remember?" Duane said. "But I still don't want to go into my house and I have no idea why you think I should marry this young woman named Anne. I just met her half an hour ago."

Ruth Popper didn't reply. For a woman in her nineties she was remarkably unlined, a fact that she attributed to her lifelong passion for crossword puzzles.

"There's nothing more relaxing than a good crossword," she often said. "A good crossword takes your mind off serious stuff, like death, for example. It's thinking bad thoughts that gives a woman lines."

"Duane, are you still being counseled by Jody Carmichael's daughter?" she asked.

"Yes—I hope I am," Duane said.

"Then can't you ask her to explain why you won't go into your own house even long enough to take a shower?" Ruth asked.

"She hasn't explained it because I haven't admitted it to her," Duane said. "Anyway, I know why I don't like to go into my own house—it's because I miss all the people who used to live there—the kids and the grandkids and even Rag."

Rag, now dead, had been the family cook. She had never been easy to get along with but she *was* the family cook.

"A person who would miss Rag is a person who is barely hanging on to his sanity," Ruth told him. "You go along now, Duane. I want to watch my shows."

3

DUANE STOPPED for a few minutes at the Kwik-Sack, where he bought a dozen eggs, a pound of bacon, some coffee, a small bottle of Cutty Sark, and three packages of small crumbly doughnuts with powdered sugar on them. As he pedaled slowly out of Thalia, on the dirt road that led to his cabin, he began to regret not having mentioned to his psychiatrist, Honor Carmichael, that he had developed an aversion to his house in Thalia. It would be at least two weeks before he *could* mention it to Honor because she and her lover Angie Cohen were vacationing in Maine for the month of August. Angie Cohen's family owned an island off the Maine coast. Honor's eccentric father, Jody Carmichael, who ran a crossroads convenience store at a dusty intersection in the oil patch some eight miles from Duane's cabin, informed him that owning an island off the coast of Maine meant that not only were Angie's family very rich, but had *been* rich for a long time.

"Department stores—big department stores—and *old* department stores," Jody said, before turning back to his computer. Jody's passion was for computer gambling, at the moment mainly involving South American soccer teams.

Duane had spent all of his sixty-four years of life in the Texas oil patch, where being super-rich usually meant that someone in the family had found a lot of oil. The wildcatter H. L. Hunt, for example, had found a lot of oil, so much oil that at one time it would have seemed almost impossible for any of his children to go broke; and yet a few of his sons achieved the near-impossible: they had gone broke, or at least came close enough to being broke that their decline made the news.

Duane kept up with financial affairs well enough to know that other kinds of businesses now made people super-rich. Bill Gates of Microsoft was now worth more than any oilman, unless you counted the Saudis. Duane was surprised to learn that an old-fashioned business such as a department store could make Angie Cohen's family rich enough to buy an island, but maybe, as Jody had suggested, they started early. Jody Carmichael might not have had a haircut in six or seven years, but he was a man who usually knew what he was talking about. Duane had now been to Egypt, but he had never been to New England and was happy enough to take Jody's word for how things worked up there.

As he pedaled over the low shaley hill to his cabin Duane began to experience a buildup of anxiety. He even hyperventilated a little, out of the sudden fear that his aversion to his house in Thalia might have spread to his cabin—the simple structure that Karla had called his "hut."

Though she had been forced to accept the reality of the hut on the hill, she had never for a moment softened toward it or admitted that Duane might derive some benefit from being in it and being alone. To Karla's way of thinking, Duane belonged in only one place, their big house, where she, and sometimes their children, and sometimes their grandchildren, lived. In Karla's view a resistance to the normal circumstances and duties of domestic life had somehow afflicted Duane—it was a virus of some sort, an anti-domestic virus that had attacked Duane and driven him out to his accursed hut.

As Duane approached his cabin he wondered where in the

world he would find to live if he no longer felt at peace in his cabin. But even before he went into the cabin and unpacked his few groceries his rising anxiety began to ebb. The sun was not quite down—there was promise of a long summer afterglow. Only one or two stars were visible yet, but soon there would be many. Once it grew really dark the Milky Way with its millions of stars would be right over his head.

The cabin was dusty, though not as dusty as Cairo. He had happened to hit Egypt on a windy week. Dust obscured the Nile, though not the pyramids. Once or twice, walking in sandstorms near the American University, it seemed to Duane that he might as well be on the campus of Texas Tech, in Lubbock, on a day when everyone was being peppered with West Texas sand.

Still, sand or no sand, he had managed to make his way to Giza, where, a lone tourist amid countless tour groups, he looked at the Great Pyramid and felt absolute awe for the first time in his life. In their one and only family outing Duane and Karla and the four kids had gone to the Grand Canyon, and Duane had been impressed, even though both Julie and Nellie had managed to get food poisoning in Flagstaff, making it far from an ideal trip. But the Grand Canyon was a work of nature while the pyramids were the works of man—certainly the most stupendous works of man that Duane had ever seen.

The cabin, to his great relief, still felt like his proper home. A small rattlesnake, about a foot long, with only a button for his tail so far, was crawling around near the stove. Duane grabbed a broom and eased the little rattler out the door.

"I'd let you stay but one of us might get careless," he said, apologetically. He didn't mind snakes, but sometimes snakes minded people.

The little rattler, making good speed, slithered under some rocks near the edge of the hill.

By then the sun was down and the western sky ablaze with

molten afterglow. It had been mainly the fine bright Texas skies that Duane had missed in Egypt—a country that he felt sure had fine skies of its own.

Once, at dawn, he had even seen the Nile under a fine sky, but then the wind came up and Cairo soon looked Lubbock-like again.

4

DUANE RARELY SLEPT long or deeply anymore. Earlier in life, when he was likely to have done a certain amount of hard physical labor, he was sometimes able to sleep deeply, but, even then, he rarely slept long. Five hours' sleep seemed to be plenty. The one time that pattern changed was in the first weeks of his therapy with Honor Carmichael—Duane discovered that talking about himself four hours a week was more tiring than any work he had done in his life. Once, after therapy, he had barely been able to bicycle back to his motel. After another session—he was then mostly living in the bridal suite of a dingy, low-grade Seymour Highway motel—he had stretched out on the water bed and slept almost around the clock, something he had never done in his entire adult life.

At his cabin, on warm nights, if he was unable to sleep, Duane usually found that he liked being outside rather than inside, and he had provided himself with a cheap but comfortable lawn chair for that purpose.

On the night of his return, once he saw that sleep wasn't going to come, he went outside and settled into his lawn chair. To the north he could see the not-very-distant lights of Wichita Falls. There were cattle on the property—Dickie and his sisters were affluent enough to dabble in the cattle business—but the cattle, wherever they were, were quiet, and likewise the coyotes, though he knew he would hear from the latter when dawn began to redden the eastern sky.

The only sounds he heard were the chug-chugs of two oil rigs, behind him and over the ridge a mile or two to the west. Very likely they were his own rigs, running all night, as usual. The fact that the only sounds disturbing the deep peace of the summer night came from his own rigs made him feel slightly annoyed—how nice it would be if he could just sit on his hill and enjoy the silence. But he had been an oilman all his life and knew that the oil business was a 24/7 boom-and-bust business: no driller in his right mind would shut down an active rig because the sound of the motors irritated Duane Moore. Most good drillers had long since forgotten what real silence *felt* like—it was just not an important factor in their lives.

In a little while the distant, monotonous chuggings of the unseen but not-too-distant rigs began to make him drowsy. The lawn chair was really a pool-or-patio chair, meaning that it could be made to lie flat. Duane lay back, drowsy, the brilliance of the Milky Way directly over his head, and went to sleep, only to awaken, after not too long, to a hazy dream of nipples. He heard a female voice say what Anne Cameron had said to him about her own nipples only that afternoon: hard as little pickles. But the nipples Duane was dreaming about were not like pickles at all: they were more like ripe raspberries, engorged with juice. The woman in his dream had smallish breasts—Anne's had also been small—and yet Duane could not put a face to the breasts. Then he seemed to catch a glimpse of pink labia, with a tuft of brownish pubic hair about the inviting slit.

Still in darkness, he awoke with an erection, hard enough to be a little painful. He loosened his pants, but, even as he freed the erection, it began to subside. He wanted to see more of the woman with the pink cunt and raspberry nipples, but the dream swiftly left him. Just at the end of it he seemed to see Honor Carmichael's face for a moment, but not her breasts and not her cunt.

The dream and the erection were both surprises. Duane had not had sex since Karla's death, two years before—he could remember only one or two erections or wet dreams during that time, although nocturnal erections had been a commonplace event throughout much of his adulthood.

But now there he was, on his hill, in the dark half hour before first light, with a subsided erection that had followed upon a dream of raspberry nipples.

Soon the coyotes began to yip. The eastern horizon reddened. Duane went inside, made himself some coffee, and ate a whole package of the crumbly little doughnuts with powdered sugar on them.

The sexy dream made Duane realize that maybe he had something new to think about: his need for a woman. Ruth Popper, irritating as she could be, was not necessarily wrong in her thinking. Karla was dead; she would not be back. He knew that he was in love with Honor Carmichael—he had even told her so—but Honor had politely shrugged him off. She had a lover, one that she was evidently quite content with.

Despite that fact, Duane knew that he was not likely to be entirely out of love with Honor for quite some time. He was free, though he didn't want to be; he would just have to see how long his attachment to Honor Carmichael lasted. He couldn't just switch his affections because a lively young woman with perky nipples and good degrees had suddenly turned up in his office in Thalia.

How exactly *that* had come about was something he wanted to find out. He kept up with oil industry developments well enough to know that the drilling and production histories of practically every oil well in the world would soon be brought online, making it possible for companies such as his to decide which wells might be worth revisiting, and which weren't. He and Dickie had more than once talked about hiring someone with geological smarts and computer savvy to take a look at the histories of the nearly two thousand wells the company had drilled over four decades. Apparently, while he was in Egypt, Dickie had acted on the notion, and had somehow persuaded a young woman upscale enough to drive a Lexus to come to Texas to work for them.

He wondered, briefly, if Dickie and Anne were lovers, and decided it was unlikely. Dickie had often been unfaithful to his somewhat spacey wife, Annette; he was always flushing short-term girlfriends out of rodeo arenas or honky-tonks—but what was certain was that none of them had degrees from MIT or Caltech. Most of the women, like Dickie himself, had no degrees at all. A California girl who didn't wear a bra and had degrees from two first-rate schools would not seem to be Dickie's cup of tea.

On the other hand, people will fool you. It had been one of Karla's favorite maxims.

"People will fool you, Duane . . . they just will," she had told him many times over the long course of their marriage.

Duane himself had proved Karla's point in spades by parking his pickup one day, after which he insisted on walking or biking everywhere he went, a decision that infuriated Karla more than anything he had done during their forty-year marriage.

"You said it yourself, honey—people will fool you," Duane told her, cheerfully.

"Duane, I didn't happen to want you to fool me," Karla said, before bursting into tears.

5

IT WAS ONLY about fifteen miles along dirt roads from Duane's cabin on the hill to the new offices of Moore Drilling on the Seymour Highway in Wichita Falls. If he got up and started Duane knew he could easily bike in before the heat got too bad. Though he had an office of his own, within the general office, he didn't stay in his office much, there being, really, nothing for him to do. Everyone deferred to him, including Dickie, and the secretaries were always plying him with not-very-good coffee, which didn't change the fact that he had nothing to do.

When, two years before, he had abruptly turned the company over to Dickie, he only half expected the transfer to work. Dickie was only a month out of rehab and had a long history of soon relapsing back into cocaine addiction. Usually he stayed clean three or four months and then started using again—he would get worse for a while and then voluntarily put himself back in rehab. He had spent nearly ten years repeating that pattern, and no one seriously expected him to break it—not Duane, not Karla, not Dickie's wife, Annette, nor any of their three children, Loni, Barbi and Sami.

But this time Dickie fooled them. He *did* break the pattern. Dickie had never lacked for energy, or ability either; he had just never bothered to apply himself to the oil business. Then he switched focus and *did* apply himself vigorously to the oil business, to the dismay of many of the employees, who discovered that they were now expected to work a great deal harder than they had been accustomed to working. Some quit—but Moore Drilling paid top dollar, and most of the old hands soon sheepishly drifted back.

All this was good: son had succeeded father and done well with the company. Now Dickie was looking hard at the potential of natural gas. Big fields were being opened in the Texas Panhandle and across the line in western Oklahoma. Dickie had talked to Duane about it a couple of times, since it would involve borrowing some money to invest in new equipment. Dickie, who had lived his life in blue jeans, was soon wearing ties and having lunch with bankers.

Duane considered pedaling over to the office just to check his mail; he got as far as filling his water bottle and going out to his bike; but, before he could straddle his bike, the feeling of aversion he had felt while standing on the back steps of his big house in Thalia rose up in him, stopping him cold. He stood by his bicycle, looking off the hill. The day was getting hotter by the minute—if he didn't go soon he would lose the morning coolness. What was the matter with him? It wouldn't have killed him to go into his house for ten minutes, long enough to shave and shower; and it wouldn't kill him to pedal over to Wichita Falls and let the folks in the office know he was back. Everyone in the office would be glad to see him, if only mildly. He was, in the secretaries' eyes, a nice old geezer who never made them snap to and do all the things they were supposed to do.

So what was wrong now? He was home, he was rested, he had seen the pyramids, it felt good to be back to his cabin: why this sudden reluctance to enter either his home or his office?

He told himself that he was being silly. He started to straddle his bike, again—then, again, he stopped. He stood by the bike for several minutes, in a state of acute indecision. The August heat was rising rapidly by then. He needed to go, if he was going—if he wasn't going he needed to give up and do something else. But what?

He remembered that Thalia was only six miles away. His visit with Anne Cameron had been very brief; he had asked her nothing. He had not even asked why the wells he had drilled in Young County in the 1970s were of particular interest to her—it was a legitimate professional question that might have broken the ice between them. But he had merely allowed himself to be surprised by her Lexus and her nipples. He made an excuse and left.

He found himself wondering if Anne would be wearing a see-through shirt again today. He had not actually seen a woman's nipples in a long time; he had really stopped thinking about sexual things until Anne Cameron surprised him. Perhaps some natural period of mourning for Karla had passed—he had no need to feel guilty about sexual thoughts, or even sexual actions, anymore.

A moment later he straddled his expensive bicycle and was pedaling at a brisk pace along the dirt road toward Thalia.

6

No Lexus was parked at the office when Duane came pedaling up. Ruth Popper's ancient Buick was there, and Bobby Lee's battered Toyota pickup—of course it was still early by Thalia standards. Duane didn't even know where Anne Cameron lived—probably she had taken an apartment in Wichita Falls, which would be the sensible thing to do.

"She's not here," Ruth Popper informed him, the minute he stepped in the door. "She won't be here today—you just wasted a trip to town."

"What is she babbling about?" Duane asked Bobby Lee—though he knew exactly what Ruth was implying.

"She's talking about the new girl with the pointy tits," Bobby Lee said. "Your bride to be, according to some people, at least."

"I don't have a bride to be," Duane said. "You're the one with the fresh bride—didn't you just marry a girl named Jessica?"

"Don't mention Jessica or he'll start bawling," Ruth said. "It's a tragic story and I don't need to hear it for the twentieth time."

"Can't you just do your crosswords and let us alone?" Bobby Lee asked. He was chewing on a matchstick and did not seem to be close to tears. In fact he seemed to be in a fairly good humor, though, as Duane knew from long experience, that could change in the blink of an eye. Since the loss of his left testicle due to cancer some years earlier, Bobby Lee had been, to say the least, emotionally volatile; his prosthetic replacement for the lost ball had not turned out to be every woman's cup of tea.

"Jessica has taken up with Darren Connor, remember him?" Bobby Lee asked.

"I do, how come he's out of jail?" Duane inquired. A few years earlier his daughter Julie had been involved with Darren Connor, who, fortunately, had been jailed in Oklahoma for having robbed a filling station and beaten the proprietor nearly to death with a tire iron.

"If it's just Darren you have nothing to worry about," Duane said. "Darren will violate his parole any day now and you'll have your wife back.

"If you *want* her back, that is."

"I guess I'll figure that out if she shows up."

"Where was Jessica from—I don't believe I ever heard you say," Duane asked.

"Odessa, the worst town in Texas for a girl to be from," Bobby Lee said.

"Why's that?" Ruth asked. Sometime earlier the staff had bought Ruth a big magnifying glass that came with a little stand so Ruth could adjust it and see her crosswords more clearly. Though proud of the glass, Ruth seldom used it, preferring to peer dimly at her crosswords. That way she could write in whatever word took her fancy.

"Why's what?" Bobby Lee asked—lately his ability to concentrate had been fitful. Often he forgot his own questions before anyone could even attempt to answer them.

Duane, Earlene, Ruth and various others who had to work with Bobby thought they might be seeing the beginnings of Alzheimer's, but no one had so far mentioned that prospect to Bobby Lee himself.

"Why is Odessa the worst town in Texas for a girl to be from?" Ruth reinquired.

"It's because of the natural gas smell," Bobby Lee told her. "It comes right up through the cracks in the sidewalk. Odessa girls grow up smelling it and it makes them real snarly."

"Where's Earlene?" Duane asked. Being in his old office was beginning to depress him, and might have depressed him more if Earlene had been there—nonetheless he felt he ought to inquire.

"Hospital, gallbladder," Ruth said. "She won't be back until next week."

"If your wife has really taken up with Darren Connor why are you so calm?" Duane asked. "Why don't you just go shoot the son-of-a-bitch? It'd be a service to the county and the state."

"I'm not a very good shot," Bobby Lee admitted. "Remember that time I tried to shoot a bug and shot my toe off instead?"

Ruth began to cackle. "I remember," she said. "You came walking in with that bloody foot and Earlene fainted and fell into the water cooler. As I recall she had to have quite a few stitches."

Then she stopped and looked at Duane.

"That was the day you parked your pickup and upset the whole town, particularly Karla," she said.

Duane vaguely remembered the shot-off little toe—by no means the most self-destructive thing he had known Bobby Lee to do. It *had* occurred on the day he parked his pickup and became a walker. But he didn't want to discuss any of that with Ruth and Bobby Lee. He didn't want to discuss anything with either of them. In fact he had begun to regret that he had even come to town. A day or two of reflection on his hill was what he needed. After all, he *had* been all the way to Egypt and back.

"Where is Anne?" he asked.

"Oklahoma City," Bobby Lee said. "She and Dickie went up to some kind of conference. An oil and gas conference, or something."

"I've been to one or two of those," Duane said. "They always have a big one about this time of year."

"I bet you're glad that you retired," Bobby Lee ventured. "Now you won't have go running around to conferences."

"He's *not* glad that he retired," Ruth countered. "Being retired just means being left out—especially to a big shot like Duane. Going to conferences in Big D or Oklahoma City or somewhere sure beats riding around on a bicycle in this heat, if you ask me."

"He didn't ask you," Bobby Lee pointed out, but it was a light, almost automatic dissent. Whatever Ruth said, Bobby Lee contradicted—and vice versa. It was exactly the kind of argument he had expected to hear when he walked into the office yesterday. Having Anne Cameron talk about her nipples—even though it startled him—was a lot more interesting.

"What are you thinking, Duane?" Ruth asked. "I know you're thinking something."

"I *was* thinking something," Duane said. "I was thinking we've all been in this town too long."

The remark seemed to startle both Ruth and Bobby Lee.

Before they could think of a comment, Duane went out the door.

7

SINCE IT WAS so close by, Duane decided to take a look at the garden plot behind his house. He and Karla had always gardened—people whose people had been through the Depression always gardened, a tradition he and Karla enjoyed carrying on. When she was killed Duane put much effort into creating what he called the Karla Laverne Moore Memorial Garden. The produce grown was free to anyone who wanted to take it. For one growing season Duane had, by common consent, the best garden ever grown in Thalia. People drove from as far as one hundred miles away to marvel at the Karla Laverne Moore Memorial Garden. They took home a little kale, or a few tomatoes, corn, snap peas, onions, or whatever took their fancy. They were very respectful— no one abused the privilege they had been offered. Poor people on the low side of the poverty line came fairly often. The poor folks were nervous about coming so often—but Duane told them not to be. The garden was so large and various that even if they came every day what they took would hardly make a dent in the abundance.

In the second year, though, Duane's impulse had flagged. He didn't plant as much as he had planted in the first year—and he hadn't tended it as well. He was slow to respond to an increase in grasshoppers. The garden was still a fine garden, but it wasn't the extraordinary garden it had been the first year.

Now of course it was August. The garden was burned to a crisp—it was time to plow it under and hope that when planting time rolled around he would find fresh inspiration and be able to produce a really exceptional garden again.

With the garden on his mind he had zipped past his house without giving it much of a glance, though he did notice that the lawn needed mowing. A local boy was supposed to see to the lawn—evidently he needed prodding. As he drove past the large empty garage on the south side of the house he noticed to his surprise that the garage wasn't entirely empty: a chocolate brown Mercedes coupé was parked in it. His daughter Julie drove a chocolate brown Mercedes coupé—perhaps she was home, though nobody at the office had mentioned having seen her, which probably meant that Julie had decided to bypass Ruth and Bobby Lee on her visit.

The big garage had once held eight cars. With only one parked in it, the place had a lonely look.

He and Julie had always been close: in his memory of parenthood, girls had been easy, boys hard. While crossing the Atlantic on the freighter, it occurred to him that his children had sort of skipped a stage—the stage of maturity that most people experienced between age twenty and age forty. They had passed from adolescence straight into middle age. The mere fact that all his children were now in their forties was a shocking thing in itself. In the young adult years all four of them had occupied themselves with drugs and dubious lovers—usually both at the same time. And yet, somehow, the girls had righted themselves and made what, so far, appeared to be stable marriages to nice, wealthy, ambitious men. Dickie had taken over the oil company successfully, and Jack, the lone rambler, was in the Alaskan Arctic, doing what nobody knew.

Duane glanced once more at the Mercedes and pedaled away; but, at the first intersection, he swung the bike around in a big curve and went back—what was he thinking of, to ride off from his own daughter without even giving her a hug? The thought crossed his mind that Julie might be there with a lover, and might not want to see anybody from Thalia. But he was not anybody: he was her father. If a lover was involved, so be it.

The back door was unlocked, so Duane eased inside.

"Honey?" he said. Then he saw Julie, in a bathing suit, playing solitaire at the kitchen table. Her hair was wet, but she jumped up at once, and gave him a warm smile and a big hug.

"I quit smoking, Daddy," she said, while they were hugging. "That one big victory to report. How were the pyramids?"

"They're amazing," Duane said. "You and Goober and the kids ought to go see them for yourselves."

"I should have gone sooner—it's too late now," Julie said.

Duane was surprised. Julie was forty-three or thereabouts: why would it be too late for a trip to the pyramids?

"I don't understand—is somebody sick?" he asked.

Julie shook her head and turned back to her card game.

"We're healthy as horses," she said. "The reason it's too late for the pyramids is that I'm going into a convent. I'm going to be a nun."

Duane was so startled that he flinched.

"Honey, did I hear you right?" he asked. "You're going to be a *nun?*"

"You heard correctly," Julie said. The firm set of her jaw reminded him of her mother.

"Want some sun tea?" she asked. "I just made some."

"I'll take a glass—do you mind if I sit down?"

"Daddy, sit down—it's your house," Julie reminded him.

Duane sat down and drank his tea.

8

WHEN HONOR CARMICHAEL, Duane's psychiatrist, finally returned from her vacation in Maine, Julie's decision to become a
nun was the first thing he mentioned in his first session. He had
supposed he would talk about his trip to Egypt, and maybe a little
about Anne Cameron, the young woman with the bold nipples,
who had come to work for Moore Drilling as a geological analyst.
But, before he knew it, the session was almost over and he had
mainly talked about his daughter's determination to enter a convent in Kentucky, a long way, in his opinion, from where her children were being raised.

Honor Carmichael said almost nothing in the session. When
he expressed his worry about the effect of Julie's decision on her
two teenage children, Willy and Bubbles, she made no response. If
anything, Honor seemed depressed herself. She usually smiled;
this time she didn't.

"Lots of women enter convents, Duane," Honor said, when
the session had only a minute or two to run. "It gets men out of
their lives, which is often a benefit."

"I guess," he said.

"It's a benefit," she insisted. "Do you remember what you were
seeking the day you parked your pickup and walked out to your
cabin for the first time?

"Gosh," he said. "I don't really know what I was seeking. I just remember that it felt good to be by myself."

"Did it feel peaceful?"

"Real peaceful."

"Then maybe peace is what you were seeking then and what your daughter's seeking now."

"Could we go back to four sessions a week, at least for a while?" he asked.

"No, we can't, Duane!" Honor said, with something like anger in her voice.

Honor stood up—she didn't smile.

"Sorry," Duane said. "Sorry."

Then he let himself out the door.

9

ONCE IN A WHILE Ruth Popper liked to make Duane dinner—
always round steak, cream gravy, pinto beans, fried okra, and corn
on the cob when it was in season. Once or twice a year she would
even invite Bobby Lee to these dinners. With the three of them
there much gossip was exchanged and conversation rarely
flagged.

Slowly, over the last year or two, Duane had begun to actually
cook the dinners himself, since Ruth was blind enough to be a little uncertain around the stove. The round steak might be as raw
as if it had just been sliced off the animal, and the gravy might be
little more than warmed-over milk. Ruth sliced the okra, which
gave her the comfortable illusion that she had actually prepared
the meal.

"I've been greedy all my life," she remarked, on this occasion.
The sun had set—the three of them ate off a small table on Ruth's
screened-in porch.

"We know that, why bring it up?" Bobby Lee asked.

"I'm trying to explain to Duane why his daughter wants to be
a nun," Ruth snapped. "She's tired of material things. She's been
living in North Dallas over a year, and she's probably out shopping
nine days out of ten. All day, year in and year out, buying things

she doesn't need and that nobody needs. Why not be a nun and sing hymns instead."

"Nuns don't sing hymns, Ruth," Bobby Lee said. "They mainly just chant them dumb old chants."

"Julie told me she never enjoyed sex," Duane said, as he was ladling out the gravy. He was mildly annoyed with the other two for rattling on. He wanted them to appreciate the gravity of the situation.

"And that's not all," he said. "As soon as she's trained she wants to be sent to El Salvador or somewhere in Central America."

"Whoa, that's not good—the death squads down there like nothing better than to shoot a few nuns," Bobby Lee said.

"That's why I'm worried," Duane said.

"How'd the sex part come up?" Bobby Lee asked. "I remember when Julie was bouncing her little butt off so many pickup seats that you and Karla thought she might be kind of a nympho."

"I'm not surprised she doesn't like sex," Ruth said. "I always suspected that about her."

Duane almost dropped the bowl of gravy.

"*You* always suspected it?" he asked.

"Don't take that tone with me—I do know a few things," Ruth said. "And pass the gravy."

"If you suspected it I wish you'd mentioned it," Duane said. "We did think maybe she liked sex too much."

"No, *I* liked sex too much—it was my downfall," Ruth said.

Bobby Lee dropped his steak knife.

"I'm not going to be able to digest my food if we don't stop talking about sex," he said. "*I* happen to like sex, but what good's it ever going to do me?"

"I doubt that either of you men ever really liked sex—I mean just pure messy old fucking," Ruth said.

"Ruth, you said the F-word," Bobby Lee said. "I come over here to eat a Christian meal and now a ninety-five-year-old woman's throwing around the F-word. Maybe the Holy Rollers are right after all. Maybe the world *is* coming to an end."

There was a little pond behind Ruth's house, from which the first chirpings of frogs were beginning to be heard. As they watched a great blue heron settled majestically at the edge of the pond.

"That heron comes by most nights," Ruth said. "Otherwise that pond would be solid frogs."

Duane applied himself to the round steak and gravy, plus two tomatoes, some cucumber slices, and crisp-fried okra. He felt deeply frustrated. Julie said her sister, Nellie, was willing to board Willy and Bubbles. Nellie had four kids of her own, so there'd be lots of cousin-support. But, for Duane, nothing was as he had thought it to be. When Julie told him she had never really liked sex, she told it as matter-of-factly as if she were saying she had never really liked spinach.

Julie was a beautiful woman. Most of the young men in and around Thalia had been in love with her at one time, a fact Duane reminded her of.

"I know," Julie said. "I suppose I encouraged them, the fools. I fucked a zillion of them but the most I ever felt was fond."

Then she informed him that her large husband, Goober Flynn, was gay.

"He's a nice man, really," Julie said. "And he's very supportive of my being a nun."

All this Duane wanted to tell Ruth and Bobby Lee, and yet, before he could get his revelations out, Ruth, who always managed to be the center of attention, began to shock both her guests with revelations of her own.

"Everybody thought I was just the mousy little coach's wife," she said. "They thought a little affair with Sonny Crawford was the best I could do—Sonny, by the way, was the worst lover I ever had. He was a really terrible fuck."

"I don't want to know none of this," Bobby Lee said. "I always had the hots for Julie myself, but I knew it was out of the question. Now I find out she wouldn't have liked it even if I had managed to get her."

"Shut up, I'm talking," Ruth said. "My second lover was Lester, you know."

"Lester Marlow?" Duane and Bobby Lee said, in chorus. Lester was the local banker, or had been. Everybody pitied his loyal wife, Jenny, because Lester himself was such an awkward clown. During the boom of the 1970s there had been an embezzlement scandal. Lester had narrowly escaped time in the pen. He had been forced to resign from the bank and puttered around going to garage sales and selling his finds at the big flea market in Fort Worth.

"It was when Lester was desperate that we started doing it on that cot in my garage," Ruth said. "There was something about how desperate he was that made it work. But Jennie caught us and we had to stop—Lester couldn't afford to have Jennie divorce him. That's when I snagged the Methodist preacher. There's nothing like screwing a preacher, if you ask me. It just felt absolutely dirty and hot, you know?"

"Well, lucky you, Ruth," Bobby Lee said, with some bitterness. "Sounds like you have had the best sex life of any of us."

"I had a decent sex life," Duane said—he regretted the words before they were well out of his mouth.

"Duane, there's no such thing as a decent sex life," Ruth said. "The whole point of fucking is that it's not decent."

"If I hear you say the F-word one more time I'll scream," Bobby Lee said.

"These are modern times, you know," Ruth said. "Old ladies can say the F-word if they want to."

"I'm glad Karla's dead," Duane said. "If she'd known one of her own daughters didn't like sex it would just about have ruined her life."

He and Bobby Lee did the dishes, while Ruth rocked in her rocking chair and listened to the chorus of frogs. Ruth couldn't see well enough to get her plates really clean. Sometimes Duane would take a plate out of Ruth's cabinet and find various food-stuffs stuck to it.

There was a sound from the porch.

"I hope she didn't fall," Duane said.

When the two of them went back to the porch to say good night they saw Ruth Popper sprawled dead on the floor, her head almost touching the screen of the porch.

"Oh my God!" Bobby Lee said. "The F-word one minute and the next minute dead."

The local clinic was two blocks away and Duane called it, but he knew Bobby Lee was right. Between one breath and another, more or less, Ruth Popper had departed.

Duane felt a certain relief—he wasn't quite sure why.

10

RUTH HAD REQUESTED only a graveside service, which was held on a day when the wind was so hot it almost raised blisters on the skin. Only about a dozen people were there. Anne Cameron, wearing a simple black dress, stood a little apart from the group. The simple black dress made her look a lot better dressed than anyone else at the funeral, or anyone else in Thalia, for that matter.

Bobby Lee, whom Duane had never seen in a tie before, had on a bright yellow one.

"I figure Ruth wouldn't have wanted me to dress gloomy," Bobby Lee said.

"You're safe then—you didn't dress gloomy," Duane said.

Lester Marlow was there, but not Jenny. When they sang "Rock of Ages," Lester cried. Duane and Bobby Lee had about decided that Ruth's romance on a cot with Lester Marlow had been some kind of old lady's fantasy, but they had to revise their opinion when they saw big tears coursing down Lester's cheeks.

"Gosh, if she had been dishing it out all during the boom I don't know why she didn't just seduce me. There was plenty of times during that boom when I could have used the pussy."

Both of Duane's daughters stayed away—neither of them had particularly liked Ruth Popper; but, rather to his surprise, both of his sons-in-law came: Goober Flynn and Zenas Church. Since neither of them knew Ruth he wondered why they had bothered to come from Dallas in such heat. Zenas had a pilot's license and flew them in his Cessna, but, still, it was an unexpected effort.

The Methodist preacher whom Ruth claimed to have had such a hot, dirty time with had come back from his retirement home in Oklahoma to perform the brief service. He hobbled up to the pulpit in his walker and mumbled a few words that no one could hear. Earlene Jacobs, who had fought bitterly with Ruth for forty years, produced a lot of loud sobs.

The grass in the grim little cemetery was burned to a golden crisp by the August heat. The graveyard was on the edge of a low bluff. Duane walked to the bluff to be alone for a few minutes. Earlene's sobbing, the preacher's walker and Bobby Lee's yellow tie combined to bring his spirits even lower than they had been; and they hadn't been high.

He walked over a few yards to Karla's grave. The little box he had made himself—really his first effort as a woodworker—with his letter to Karla in it, was where he had placed it, in front of the gray monument. He had put it there as he was leaving for Egypt— that had been only about two weeks ago, and yet, in a mere two weeks, Thalia had seemed to have become bleaker, hotter, dustier, and more sparsely peopled than it had been the day he left. The laundrymat had closed, and the biggest local insurance company had, like Moore Drilling, relocated to Wichita Falls. Not only had he outlived his own wife, and Ruth Popper—it seemed to Duane that he had sort of outlived the town of Thalia itself. All the stores the locals really needed—Wal-Mart, Target, Office Max, a twenty-four-hour Albertson's—were right there on the south side of Wichita Falls, barely fifteen minutes by pickup from where he stood. It seemed to him that there could only be less and less need for Thalia, Texas, as a town. A few old-timers such as Lester Marlow, Bobby Lee and himself would stick it out; but his children had already left and it was unlikely that even his grandkids would bother coming to Thalia for more than a weekend now and then, maybe in hunting season. They were city kids now—and just as well. He himself wasn't a city person, and didn't really want to try and learn to be one, which meant, probably, that he would pedal from cabin to town to suburb, growing lonelier and older, as the people he had lived his life with continued to die, or else move into retirement homes in Wichita Falls. When he looked back at Thalia from the graveyard there already seemed to be less of it.

Deep in regret, Duane did not notice when Anne Cameron walked up to him and gave his hand a gentle squeeze.

"Penny for your thoughts, Mr. Moore," she said.

"They're not worth a penny," he said. "I was just thinking what a miserable, windblown drying-up town this is."

"It's a hole all right," Anne said.

"But you came here," he said. "Why on earth did you let Dickie talk you into it?"

"By offering me a good chunk of money that I can make quick—our deal is for six months, no more," she said. "After that I'm going to Indonesia, to do roughly the same thing for a larger company. I figured I could stand anything for six months."

"I suppose if you're good enough with that computer you can work anywhere," he said.

"That's right," Anne said. "And I'm good enough."

"How are the little pickles?" he asked—his own comment shocked him. He had probably never made a bolder statement to a woman in his life. Desperation made him say it. He had a vision of how much he was going to hate it when Anne Cameron left for Indonesia.

She didn't seem surprised by the remark; she looked at him directly.

"This is a funeral," she said. "No tittie action today. You're being a little naughty, seems to me."

She walked away, said a word or two to Bobby Lee, and proceeded to her Lexus.

The casket was being lowered when Bobby Lee strolled over, taking off his yellow tie.

"Where did Dickie find Annie?" Duane asked. "How would he know how to find someone like her?"

"Chat-boards," Bobby Lee told him. "Oil industry chat-boards. That's how people find other people now, Duane. You're behind the times."

"Way behind the times," Duane said.

11

WHEN HE SAW Anne Cameron drive away in her green Lexus, Duane's spirits, low enough to begin with, sank lower still. Why in God's name had he asked Anne Cameron about her nipples at a funeral? Of course she herself had called attention to them the day before—but that might have just been a moment of girlish playfulness. But for him to have mentioned them at Ruth Popper's funeral was a big error—and a confusing one. She had squeezed his hand in a friendly way and he had responded coarsely, although he had almost never been coarse in his dealings with women.

What it meant, he supposed, was that he had been alone and sexless so long that he had forgotten the language of women—a language that involved hints and smiles and necklines that might show a little bosom. Duane realized that he no longer knew how to approach a woman he wanted to seduce. After all, he had made two attempts to kiss Honor Carmichael and Honor, though polite, had clearly not taken him seriously as a would-be lover.

He had the lowering feeling that young Anne Cameron wouldn't take his advances seriously either—if he made any. Standing in the hot wind, as Ruth's few mourners shuffled to their cars, Duane realized that he was an aging man who had long since forgotten how to get women he was interested in to go to bed with him. Even in his last years with Karla there had been practically no sex, a fact that was probably more his fault than hers. Karla had complained bitterly about his inattention, though he suspected that that complaint had been made mainly for the sake of complaint. With three kids and most of the grandkids living with them in the big house, domestic chaos tended to quash desire. For the two of them to isolate sexual desire long enough to strip off and actually make love was a rare thing.

He had gone into his house and put on a suit for the funeral, and was just about to mount his bike and pedal back to the house and take the suit off, when he was caught by his two sons-in-law, Zenas and Goober.

"We want to buy you lunch, Duane," Zenas said. He didn't look happy.

"Things are a little weird in Dallas—we thought you might want to be brought up to date," he added.

Duane liked both of his sons-in-law—they seemed like nice men. Goober looked no happier than Zenas—in other words, not happy at all. Of course his daughters, Julie and Nellie, had had their way with lots of men—even if Julie wanted to give up married life and go be a nun, the two sisters could still find ways to be rough on husbands.

"There's something more than the convent?" Duane asked.

"Yep," Zenas said. "Let's go to the Dairy Queen. I'll buy you a chicken-fry."

"Okay, but I want to go by the house and get out of this suit," Duane said.

A half hour later the three of them were in the Dairy Queen, staring at the three tough-as-a-boot examples of the staple food of West Texas: chicken-fried steak with cream gravy, the very dish he had served Ruth Popper just before she fell dead.

"I hate to think how many of these dried-out pieces of meat you must have eaten in your years in the oil patch," Goober said.

"Thousands," Duane assured him. "What else don't I know that I might need to know?"

"Nellie's gay—she threw me out," Zenas said.

"And I'm gay too—that is I mostly am," Zenas admitted. "Right now I have a nice boyfriend who's a high school basketball coach. But I'm really AC/DC. And, to be fair, when I say Nellie threw me out I should mention that she didn't throw me very far. I live in the guesthouse, which is pretty nice."

Duane had stayed in the guesthouse several times—a two-story guesthouse with a wall-sized TV and all the comforts of home, including a state-of-the-art barbecue.

For a moment Duane wished he could be back on the freighter *Tappan Zee,* looking down at the great green ocean.

"Nellie has a girlfriend named Bessie," Zenas said. "She manages a foundation."

None of the three had so far touched their chicken-fried steaks, though Goober had gone so far as to pepper his gravy.

"What about the kids?" Duane asked. Nellie's kids weren't by Zenas, nor Julie's by Goober, but both men seemed to have been admirable stepfathers.

"Oh, you know how kids are, nowadays," Zenas said. "They're cool with it."

"Sexual orientation is just not that big a deal, anymore, Duane—at least it isn't in the circles the kids move in," Goober said.

Duane carefully ate a bite of steak. He felt grateful to the two men—both decent men—for coming to Ruth's funeral to tell him what they had told him. Both men, usually jolly and even boisterous, were subdued and obviously anguished by the situation with his daughters. He wasn't so convinced about the kids, himself.

"How come you're not throwing *them* out?" he asked. "You're the husbands—you own the houses—or the mansions, to be accurate. Seems like my daughters have just kind of deserted you—why don't you throw them out?"

"Oh well, we still love them," Goober admitted, with a bobble in his voice. "We both feel we might as well stick around—keep an eye on things, you know. Do some carpooling for the kids—coach a little soccer."

"When did Nellie decide she was gay?"

"About eight months ago, when Bessie moved in," Zenas said. "We saw no reason to rush up and tell you—after all, it could have just been a phase."

"But now you don't think it's a phase?"

Both men shook their heads. Their faces told him plainly enough that they didn't think their wives were just going through a phase.

Duane tried to focus—to be helpful—after all, the men had flown from Dallas. He wanted to offer them some words of encouragement—but he couldn't think of any. He had been brought up not to leave food on his plate, so he slowly ate his chicken-fried steak, his green beans, his mashed potatoes—even his little salad.

Goober and Zenas were not so spartan. They left most of their food.

"It's a little like chewing wood," Goober observed.

Duane felt for a second time that it was just as well Karla was gone. She wouldn't have wanted to know that Julie had never enjoyed sex, or that Nellie had taken up with a woman named Bessie who ran a foundation.

He biked out to the little one-hangar airport and saw the men off.

"I appreciate your coming," he said. "If I can help just call."

"We appreciate your being here—you're solid and you're about the only one who is," Zenas told him.

But I'm not solid, Duane thought, as he watched the little yellow airplane nose into the white afternoon sky. Once he *had* been solid, or at least had felt solid—but not anymore.

12

DUANE BIKED past his office, saw Anne Cameron's Lexus parked there, and didn't stop. Instead he biked to his house, found a tablet and an envelope and wrote Anne a note of apology, which read:

Dear Miss Cameron:
I want to apologize for saying what I said to you at the grave-yard. It was totally inappropriate. I hope you can overlook it. I'd like to be your friend.
Duane Moore

As he was putting the note in an envelope the phone rang—caller ID told him it was Nellie, so he picked up.

"Hi, honey," he said. "What's up with you?"

"Oh well, I guess Zenas told you how things stand," Nellie said. "I suppose I should have told you myself and told you sooner."

"Are you happy?" he asked.

"I *am* happy, Daddy—I'm very happy."

"And the kids are okay about Bessie?"

"Oh, they love her, she's a sports nut," Nellie said. "She takes them to Mavericks games and keeps up with all the cool bands."

"Well, that's good," he said. "Is she your age?"

There was a pause.

"Bessie's twenty-eight," Nellie said. "That's why it's easy for her to keep up with the right bands.

"Does it upset you that I'm with a woman?"

"Not if you're happy," he said. "I think it upsets Zenas though."

"You think we're hard on men, don't you, me and Julie," Nellie said.

"Yes—but both those men are grown-ups," he said. "They can move on if they want to."

"Nope, they're hung up on us—that's part of the problem," Nellie said. "What do you think about Julie and the convent?"

"Fine—I sometimes wish I was in a monastery myself."

"You are—your cabin's your cell," Nellie said. She felt nervous. Bessie was due home any moment, and Bessie was really possessive. Even though it was only her father she was talking to, Bessie would come in wanting instant attention. If she didn't get it, she might flare up.

"Don't worry too much about Goober and Zenas," she told him. "After all, they're both good-looking millionaires. They'll do okay."

"I wish you'd bring Bessie home sometime—I'd like to meet her," Duane said.

Nellie tried to imagine herself and Bessie in Thalia, but on that one her imagination drew a blank. The two of them were so obviously attracted that even in North Dallas they occasionally drew stares. A visit to Thalia was just not in the picture—at least not anytime soon.

"Just try to talk your sister out of getting assigned to El Salvador, or anyplace else dangerous," he asked.

"We'll see, Daddy," Nellie said—then she got an anxious note in her voice. Probably her young girlfriend had just pulled in, which meant that the call was over.

Duane was just as glad. He really didn't like being in his house.

Before he left he carefully peeled all the family snapshots off the refrigerator door and put them in a drawer.

13

DUANE PEDALED BACK to his office and slipped the envelope containing his apology under the windshield of Anne Cameron's Lexus. He felt a little cowardly for taking such a formal approach—he could just have stopped into the office, which, after all, was *his* office—and apologized directly, but somehow he thought the note under the windshield was a better way to do it, mainly because he was a little intimidated by Anne Cameron, ridiculous as that seemed. She was highly educated; he had rarely set foot on a college campus and in fact had not even urged his kids to go to college—Karla hadn't either. Neither of them wanted their children to get educated above them—it was a wrong attitude in a parent and they both knew it, but, since none of their children showed the slightest interest in college it was the attitude that prevailed.

It was still windy—he wanted to make sure that the note didn't blow away. He *really* wanted Anne Cameron to see it.

While he was making the envelope secure the door opened and Anne came out. Instead of the black dress she had worn to the funeral she now wore cutoff jeans and the shirt she had worn the day Duane met her—the shirt that showed her small breasts. Her legs were long and tan.

"I bet that's a note of apology you're sticking under my wind-shield wiper," she said. "You're a strange one, Mr. Moore—why didn't you just hand it to me?—or, better yet, why didn't you just step inside and apologize?—after all, I started the whole silly nipple business, and what you said today at the funeral was not the biggest deal in the world. We both ought to be able to talk to one another about something besides tits."

"I'm ready to try," he said.

Anne Cameron regarded him silently.

"Are you always this weak with women?" she asked, unsmiling.

Duane was dumbfounded by the charge. Nobody had ever suggested to him that he was weak with women. After all, he had been married to Karla Laverne Moore for forty years—a woman half the men in Thalia were scared to death of. If he was weak with women, what about Karla?

There was a long, awkward silence. Duane considered just pedaling away, leaving Anne Cameron's question unanswered, since he realized he didn't know how to answer it. *Was* he weak with women?

Anne Cameron yielded no ground. She waited, impatience in her eyes. She folded her arms over her small breasts and waited.

"I guess I don't know the answer to that question," Duane said. "I guess I better ask my psychiatrist and see what she thinks."

"Would that be the shrink everybody says you're in love with?" she asked.

"That's the one."

"If you really ask her she's going to tell you you're weak with women," Anne said.

She stepped down off the porch and took the envelope that he had just stuck under the windshield wiper. She raised it above her head and squinted at it, as if to read it through the envelope.

When she raised her arms Duane noticed that she had a dark tuft of armpit hair. It startled him—he couldn't remember when he had seen a woman with armpit hair.

Anne Cameron noticed his reaction and regarded him with a hint of a smile.

"Oh that," she said, showing him both armpits for a moment. "That's a legacy of my French years—I hate shaving under my armpits. Ever see *Diary of a Chambermaid*? The Buñuel movie?"

Duane shook his head.

"I mentioned it because Jeanne Moreau plays the chambermaid and she didn't shave under her armpits—I thought that was *so* sexy."

Duane noticed, what he hadn't before, that Anne Cameron had green eyes.

"Maybe you're just out of practice with girls, Mr. Moore," Anne said. "If I'm feeling naughty I sometimes let my boyfriends shave my legs. It seems to be a big turn-on even for computer geeks."

She turned and went back into the office without giving Duane another glance.

14

DUANE PEDALED OUT to his cabin in a state of deep confusion. The road led past the graveyard where Ruth Popper had just been buried—he realized that, with Ruth's passing, he had lost not only a lifelong friend but also a reliable sounding board. Karla, his wife, had never been particularly reliable as a sounding board—Karla was compelled by her own agenda, which she fought for with great tenacity. She had no interest in objectivity—just in what she believed in and wanted.

Ruth Popper could be perverse. She would start out by regarding almost anything Duane said or did with skepticism—but then she would lighten up and give reasonable opinions on almost any question that he brought to her.

If he asked Ruth if he was weak with women she would take her time thinking about it, but would eventually tell him what she thought. Her ultimate fairness had served him well in many disputes over many years—and yet now, when he was more confused than he had ever been, Ruth had gone and died, leaving him without a sounding board.

For a long time—for decades—Duane had been considered the most successful man in Thalia. He had been, at various times, mayor, president of the school board, and chairman of the Chamber of Commerce. His oil company had survived both booms and busts. Moore Drilling employed more people than any other company in the county. True, it wasn't much of a county—there was still only one stoplight in the whole county. Excessive traffic was one problem that Thalia didn't have. It had drugs aplenty and oilfield theft and all manner of marital irregularity—but at least, unless there was a colossal wreck, the traffic rarely piled up.

When he left for Egypt, only about three weeks earlier, he still considered himself more or less successful. Of course his therapy with Honor Carmichael had shown him that he was not really quite what he seemed. He knew that he was confused about some things and that there were areas of pain inside him he had to be careful not to expand. But, generally, he had no reason to consider himself an out-and-out failure in his sixty-four years on earth. He had been a decent father, a decent husband, a decent citizen of his community.

Now, though, as his bike made a little dust trail along the country road, Duane found his conviction of self-worth severely shaken. For one thing he had lost his entire family to the call of other places. Karla had died in the smash-up and the rest had simply left. Of course, to be fair, most of them had left before Karla's death. Perhaps more important, it was obvious that none of them were coming back. Dickie was close by, but the other three of their children were gone. He knew he might as well put his big house on the market. He didn't want to be in it, and neither did any of his descendants. So far as the Moore *family* was concerned, Thalia was a place of the past. The family roots had been shallow to begin with—now the children had pulled them up. They were out of there.

Duane soon came to the hill where his little cabin sat, but he didn't turn into the dirt trail to his little dwelling. He felt too confused—he needed to talk to someone, if only in a mundane way about mundane things. Jody Carmichael's crossroads convenience store was only eight miles farther, so Duane kept pedaling. Jody sold fishing lures, and Duane had once been a keen fisherman. With so little to do in what he supposed was his retirement perhaps he should get back into fishing. Even if he didn't, buying a few lures would give him an excuse for the visit.

Duane was really hot by the time he reached the store. Jody's green Buick station wagon was usually parked under a good-sized sycamore tree, but today, in place of the Buick, there was a small blue Subaru pickup.

Seeing the Subaru where he had been expecting the Buick made Duane suddenly anxious. Jody had weathered various fairly serious ailments over the years. Maybe he had died; though, if he had, surely Bobby Lee would have mentioned it.

With some trepidation he parked his bike and pushed open the screen door. There was no sign of Jody Carmichael, or of the big computer he used for his computer gambling. The store was clean as a pin, though, and two small alert men the color of plums greeted Duane with smiles.

"Howdy—what happened to Mr. Jody?" Duane asked, cautiously.

The two plum-colored men kept smiling.

"He moved to Inglewood, it's in California," one of the men said.

"Play the horses," the other man said. "Mr. Jody sold the store to us."

"I'm Mike, he Tommy," he added. "Maybe you are Mr. Moore."

"How'd you guess?"

"Mr. Jody said you would come on a bike," Tommy told him. "He said you are such a good customer we should give you a discount."

"How about ten percent?" Mike asked. Neither of them had stopped smiling.

"Well, sure—that's nice of you," Duane said. "Where are you gentlemen from?"

"Sri Lanka," Mike said. "Long way."

"I bet it is," Duane agreed.

"We have wok—we have grill," Tommy said. "Feed the oil-boys when they get off work. Spring rolls very popular with the oilboys. So is barbecue. You want some?"

Duane realized he was hungry. At the back of the store Mike and Tommy had set up up a little buffet: spring rolls, barbecued pork on skewers, shrimp dumplings, chicken wings. The food smelled delicious and, as it proved, *was* delicious. Jody Carmichael had merely provided a microwave and some packaged burritos. No wonder the oilboys liked the new Sri Lankan menu. He could not imagine how Mike and Tommy had made it from Sri Lanka to that dusty crossroads in West Texas, but it was fortunate for the oilboys that they had.

Indeed, once he had eaten and was pedaling away, three pick-ups full of his own roughnecks came barreling up to their new South Asian deli.

Mike and Tommy wanted to give their new business a name and had asked Duane to suggest something, a suggestion that left him somewhat at a loss. As far as he could recall, the little store had once been called the Corners.

"You might call it the Corners," he said, but Mike and Tommy thought that suggestion rather dull.

"We might call it Asia Wonder Deli," Tommy said. "Wonder has nice ring."

"You're right, I like it," Duane said.

"No charge," Tommy said, when Duane tried to pay for the food, of which he had eaten a healthy amount.

"We hope you come back," Tommy said. "In Sri Lanka we ride bikes too—but not here. Here too far."

"And too crazy," Mike added.

"Too crazy is right," Duane said.

15

SOMETIMES, IN THEIR SESSIONS, Honor Carmichael would talk. She was never exactly chatty, but neither was she loath to speak out when she had an important point to make about Duane's behavior or his attitude.

Other days, Honor would be completely inscrutable, listening closely but not responding. When he told her about Anne Cameron she watched him but didn't say anything. When he mentioned that Anne said he was weak with women Honor merely shrugged.

"You aren't *with* a woman and you haven't been for some time, if we don't count your office staff," Honor said.

"So it doesn't much matter whether you're weak with them or not—it could be that you're tired of women and are ready to let all that go."

"All what go?" he asked.

"Sex—romance," Honor said. "I doubt that you know much about sex, really, Duane, and unless Annie Cameron or someone like her decides to eat you for lunch you probably never will know much about sex."

"I once thought I knew something," Duane said. "I was married a long time."

Again, Honor shrugged.

"Millions of married men go through life knowing very little about sex," she said.

"Yesterday a woman told me I was weak with women," Duane said. "Today you tell me I don't know much about sex. And two Sri Lankans are running your father's quick stop and running it well. It's too much for an old country boy to take in.

"And that's not counting my daughters," he added.

"Last time you were here you said you wanted to see me four times a week," Honor said. "Is that because you're really troubled, or is it because you're still hoping to interest me romantically?"

"I'm pretty troubled," he said. "Even at the cabin I don't get the old peaceful feeling very often. I wake up anxious most days. Real anxious, sometimes."

Then he remembered that Honor had called Anne Cameron Annie—it suggested that she knew her.

But when he asked, Honor shook her head.

"Never met the girl—but I know her family," Honor said. "One of her aunts roomed with Angie at Smith, way back in the dreamtime. They're very rich Californians, the Camerons. They basically own Pasadena—or at least they did. Small world, isn't it?

"At a certain level of wealth—a high level, obviously—all the really rich people more or less know all the other really rich people. They go to the same schools, or the same spas, and have their palaces in the same impeccable places. I'm sure Angie knows a lot more about the Camerons than I do, but I don't think I'll tell her that one of Cecil Cameron's daughters is trying to seduce one of my patients."

"I don't think she has any interest in seducing me," he said.

Honor snorted.

"You walk in from Egypt and her nipples get hard," she said. "Then yesterday she shows you her sexy French armpit hair and mentions that some of her boyfriends get to shave her legs. Doesn't that strike you as seductive behavior?"

"Yet she may just be a flirt," Duane said. "After all, I'm an old codger."

Honor thought about it for a moment.

"You're not presentable socially, which, in Cameron terms, means you'd be a particularly hot fuck. To put it bluntly. But don't expect her to take you to lunch at the yacht club in Newport Beach, or Newport, Rhode Island, either."

Honor began to drum her fingers on the desk in front of her. She had seldom exhibited such restlessness in their sessions. He didn't know what it meant. Also, she seemed worried. Honor had a capacity for merriment, even mischief, that she seldom suppressed for long. But since her vacation in Maine neither the merriment nor the mischief had surfaced.

"Is something wrong?" Duane asked, after a considerable silence had grown.

"I'm supposed to ask *you* that, Duane," Honor said. "What might be wrong with me is none of your business. But I do have some advice for you. Go off and learn a little something about sex. Acquire some real skills. You might need them someday."

Duane didn't answer. His time was up. Honor politely but silently showed him out of the room.

16

BY THE TIME Honor's office door closed behind him, Duane knew he was dropping into a serious depression. The sun was merciless—at least he had left his bicycle in the shade. He felt hopelessly discouraged. What was he to do? Honor was the one woman he wanted, and she did not want him. Who would he find to help him learn whatever it was he didn't know about sex? He was sixty-four. If he hadn't learned to be a good lover by then, how likely was it that he would ever be a good lover?

At a loss, worried, sad, he pedaled to the offices of Moore Drilling. He went slow. The day was really hot.

Dickie, his son, was talking on a cell phone when he walked in—something about his father's look evidently worried Dickie so that he broke off the call.

"Daddy, you look terrible," Dickie said. "You're gray as oatmeal. What's the matter?"

"I don't know," Duane admitted. The remark about his color surprised him—he had never given a thought to his color.

"You worry me," Dickie said. "You look like you'd keel over if you had to dig a posthole, or even mow the lawn."

He quickly shut the door to his office, so he and Duane could be alone.

Duane had always been a healthy person, so much so that he had never thought of himself as anything but healthy. If he looked bad to Dickie it was probably because his intense depression showed.

"What do you think of Annie?" Dickie asked.

"I haven't seen enough of her to know what to think," Duane said. "She's prettier than Earlene, I know that."

"Well, she's going to make us richer," Dickie said. "She's going to show us old wells that could be big producers. The only reason they weren't big producers the first time around was because we couldn't get the money to go deeper. Annie's not only got the schooling for this job—she's also got the instincts."

"Reexploration—I suppose that's the trend," Duane said, though he could not really work up much interest.

"Do you ever hear from your sisters?" he asked.

"I know about Nellie being gay, and I know Julie wants to be a nun," Dickie said. "I'm more interested in you, though. You just don't look right. I doubt you should be pedaling a bike around in one-hundred-and-ten-degree heat—hell, nobody should."

"Oh, I'll take it slow until it cools off," Duane said.

Nonetheless Dickie was still looking worried as he pedaled away.

Duane's destination was the Asia Wonder Deli. He thought he might just eat a spring roll or two. He had enjoyed his few minutes with his son, but depression settled in before he was out of sight of his own offices. Duane mostly ignored heat, as he ignored cold or any other weather short of tornadoes. But he had not gone more than a mile before he began to feel that the heat had become an element in his depression. The heat suddenly surrounded him—he felt as if he were riding through a furnace; he wanted to get out of the furnace but there was no way out. The furnace wouldn't cool until sunset—perhaps wouldn't cool much even then. Soon the heat—or was it the depression—was affecting his breathing. Before he had gone three miles he knew that he had overmatched himself with the heat. Dickie was right: he shouldn't be riding a bike in one-hundred-and-ten-degree heat. He had begun to tremble; so much sweat dripped into his eyes that he could barely see. He began to wobble on his bike. He didn't know what a heat stroke felt like, but he had begun to fear he might be having one.

Fortunately he was only about two hundred yards from a little creek that had some good shade trees around it. Mike and Tommy's was out of reach, but he thought the shade trees might save him.

He was wobbling worse and worse, but he just made it to the shade trees and got off his bike, Fortunately he still had nearly a full water bottle. He drank a few swallows and poured a little of what remained over his head. The little creek, alas, was dry.

It was good to be off his bike, but he wasn't getting any cooler, and he became aware that his heart was racing. The heat was still all around him, like an invisible tent. He was trembling as hard as he had ever trembled in his life. He could not remember ever having reacted so severely from heat before. The heat and his reaction to it were so intense that he lost his feeling of depression. He realized he was just too old to have attempted what he had attempted. He wondered if he might die—a dairy farmer he knew slightly had died one day of a heat stroke, on a day about as hot as this one.

Duane sat for twenty minutes—he felt no better, but at least he didn't feel worse. In an hour it should start feeling cooler. Fortunately he still had a little water. In two hours he might be able to pedal on to Mike and Tommy's and eat a spring roll or two.

While Duane was waiting, being as still as possible, waiting for the heat to subside, he heard a pickup coming. The road it was on was rather out of the way. Only an occasional cowboy or oil-boy, to use Tommy's term, would be likely to be on it. Somehow the approaching pickup, which was still a ridge or two away, had a motor that sounded familiar. When it finally hove in sight it *was* familiar: it was Bobby Lee, in his old battered Toyota.

Bobby was smoking along at top speed, as usual, and no doubt his mind was on other things as he drove. He failed to see Duane as he sped by but just noticed the bike out of the corner of his eye; he hit his brakes and stopped, then slowly backed up until he was on a level with the bicycle. Duane stood up then, and was chagrined to find that he was even weaker and shakier than he had been when he stopped and parked his bike.

"Whoa, hoss—you're white as a sheet," Bobby said. "Why would you ride a damn bicycle when it's this hot?"

"I'll be fine," Duane said—not feeling fine at all. "Just haul me to my cabin."

"Duane, if you could see how you look I hope you'd have better sense than to even think of going to that cabin," Bobby Lee said. "For all I know you could be dying. I'm calling an ambulance."

Duane felt a momentary resistance. He had always controlled his own state of health. But the fact was, he *did* feel very strange. Bobby Lee got on his cell phone and called 911. Duane leaned against one of the shade trees. He found that, for once, he was rather glad to let Bobby Lee make a decision for him.

"It's lucky you came by, I guess," he said, weakly, "I wouldn't have made it to Mike and Tommy's. What brought you out this way?"

"Dickie said I should hurry up and find you, that's what brought me out on this miserable fucking road," Bobby informed him.

Very soon they heard the wail of the ambulance—Duane was only some four miles from his office, and still in sight of Wichita Falls. When the ambulance showed up he fell silent—he made no protest when he was put on a gurney and lifted into the cool ambulance, which, in only a few minutes, arrived at the emergency room of a big, cool hospital. Dickie showed up, and he and Bobby Lee handled all the details of Duane's admission. The sound of their voices seemed to come from a great distance. Duane knew that what they were doing was for the best. He had no doubt been foolish and had probably had a heat stroke—but somehow he felt a great disinterest in it all. It didn't seem to be happening to him, but to another man who resembled him. He mainly wanted the formalities of admittance to be over so he could take a nice long nap. A nice nap in a cool room would, he felt sure, put him right again.

"I guess I'm not as young as I used to be," he said to Bobby Lee and Dickie, as he was being wheeled along the hall to his room.

What he said was such a cliché that neither Bobby Lee nor Dickie bothered to reply.

Their silence irritated Duane a little bit. Why wouldn't they talk to him? He hadn't said anything to them particularly dumb, he didn't think. But pretty soon he was in his room and things got hectic and crowded. Two doctors showed up—both of them listened long and thoughtfully to his heart.

One of the doctors was an older man named Calvert—at one time he had been Karla's doctor. After Karla's death Duane had occasionally seen him at various civic events, but he didn't know him well. The young doctor seemed to be in charge—he introduced himself, but in Duane's half-indifferent state the name failed to stick.

"Daddy, they want to do an EKG, just to be sure your heart's all right," Dickie said.

Duane had had periodic EKGs, mostly at Karla's urging—the procedure had not been particularly onerous and his heart had always been okay, so he nodded his assent. What he wanted to do was go to sleep, but inasmuch as he was in the hospital it seemed best just to let the doctors run their tests.

Then he could get an early start in the morning and reach his cabin before it got dangerously hot.

He dozed through the EKG—he heard the doctors murmuring with Dickie, but he didn't pay a great deal of attention. When the test was over he was taken to a room and offered a meal, but he only ate a spoonful of fruit salad before drifting off to sleep. He dreamed of the ocean and of trying to set pipe in a new well in the midst of a lightning storm. All the crew ran away—he could see little flickers of blue lightning on the running men's hard hats. Then he found himself riding his bicycle across the surface of the ocean at a time of day when the sun was very bright.

Duane woke at first light, as he usually did—he had meant to check out of the hospital and pedal away, but a lassitude seized him and he continued to lie in bed. He passed on breakfast when it was offered; he began to wonder if Bobby Lee had neglected to leave him his bicycle. He felt sure he could make it to his cabin on his bike if he didn't wait too long to start. But with no bike he would be forced to hitch a ride, and then would be stuck in his cabin until Bobby Lee showed up with his bike. It was all faintly irritating, and yet the lassitude he could not seem to shake off kept him in his bed. He blamed only himself for this bump in the road—if he hadn't ignored the power of the August heat he wouldn't be off track to the extent that he was. He knew better than to try and beat nature—he had always known better—and yet he had been foolish and had done just that, only to have nature immediately slap him down.

About seven he did get up and slowly put on his clothes—just as he was about to go in search of his bike he heard footsteps in the hall and who should appear but his children: Dickie, Julie, Nellie, accompanied by the sharp-featured young doctor whose name he had forgotten.

"Good Lord, the board of governors," Duane said. "What brought this on?"

"You—we're all worried sick about you," Julie said. "You had a heart attack."

Duane was not entirely surprised by this news. Even half asleep he had been aware the night before that the doctors were not entirely pleased with his EKG. Their murmurings with Dickie had a worried tone.

"I was hoping it was just a heat stroke," he said, looking at the young doctor, who met his eye and reintroduced himself as Dr. Joel Peppard.

Duane felt mildly annoyed, as he always did, when his family descended on him in force. He knew he was wrong to feel annoyed: they were his kids, they loved him; certainly they only wanted to help. Why it was that he didn't want to be helped was a perversity that he could discuss with Honor Carmichael sometime. For the moment he was more interested in what came next, medically, and, since two of his children had driven up from Dallas he was determined to stay polite.

"All signs point to a heart attack, though a small one, I should add," Dr. Peppard told him. "There are arteries no longer than my little fingernail—one of these tiny ones may have failed—there's probably no damage to your heart muscle, if that's what happened."

It was at that moment, as Duane would later tell Honor, that his life ceased to feel like his own.

Honor at once attacked that notion.

"If you have real connections to your family, your friends, and your lovers, then your life is never more than partly your own," she said. "What next?"

"A stress test was next," he told her. "Dr. Peppard wanted me to do one before I left the hospital. He felt sure I'd pass it.

"But he was wrong—I failed it."

"Uh-oh," Honor said. She suddenly looked at him in a friendly way again, something she had not done since her vacation.

"I suppose that means you've been lucky," she said. "You haven't *had* a serious heart attack, but you can probably expect one soon. Correct?"

"That's what the doctors think," Duane said.

"And what do you think, Duane?"

"I don't feel right," Duane said. "I feel something's off. Maybe not very off, but off.

"I guess the next thing to do is get an angiogram," he went on.

"Good boy! Do it right away!"

"I guess that would be best," Duane said, though he wasn't fully convinced.

17

As Dr. Peppard and the technicians were preparing to proceed with his angiogram Duane was handed a form to sign, which told him, he just happened to notice, that the procedure he was about to undergo could be fatal. It startled him a little, since Dr. Peppard had never mentioned that possibility.

"You mean this could kill me?" he asked. "And if it can, why am I doing it?"

All three of his children were waiting in the hall: had *they* known angiograms could be fatal?

"I've never lost a patient to an angiogram," Dr. Peppard said. "It's a rare thing. But this *is* an invasive procedure and we have to inform the patient that there *is* a risk. Once in a while someone reacts negatively."

"Dying? I guess I'd call that reacting negatively," Duane told him; but he allowed the test to proceed. The odd sense of lassitude had not quite left him, nor had the strange detachment that he had felt ever since his crisis by the dry creek. He was allowed to watch the progress of the dye they shot into him on an overhead monitor. He watched the dye moving toward his heart, and yet felt mainly indifferent to what was going on. Somehow it didn't really feel like it was *him* the dye had entered. The body was his, but his spirit, if it still existed, was somewhere else.

"Uh-oh," Dr. Peppard said, staring intently at the monitor. "That's what I was afraid of."

Duane, even in his detached state, saw the problem too. The dye didn't seem to be moving through his heart.

The test was soon concluded, and he didn't die. In fact he walked out of the lab feeling, if anything, a little better, even though he had seen with his own eyes what the dye did. It stopped when it got to his heart, which meant that, though alive, he wasn't problem-free.

Dr. Peppard made his report to Duane, Dickie, Nellie, and Julie. The children looked worried. Duane, having survived a procedure that could have been fatal, was feeling like himself again.

"Daddy, why are you looking so cheerful?" Julie asked. "You've got three major arteries that are ninety percent blocked. You could keel over any day."

"I suppose it's what happens if you eat ten thousand chicken-fried steaks," he said, in an effort to inject a little humor into the proceedings. The effort failed: Nellie promptly burst into tears.

"Hey, ease up," he said. "I'm standing on my own two feet in a hospital. The doctor isn't going to let me die, I don't think."

"I'm going to try not to," the doctor said. "You must have pretty good collateral circulation, since you bike everywhere."

"Isn't there some Drano or something that could get things moving up there?" Duane asked.

"Someday we'll have the Drano, but right now we don't," Dr. Peppard said. "What we have now are scalpels. What you need in my opinion is triple bypass surgery—and you need it soon."

It was Duane's turn to be stunned.

"You mean an operation?" he asked.

"That's right."

"Then what do you mean by soon?" Duane asked.

"Tomorrow wouldn't be too soon," the doctor said, looking nervous.

"Maybe not for you but it's too soon for me," Duane said. "I'd need to do some investigating before I let anything like that happen."

"Oh, Daddy—please don't be stubborn," Julie said, too loudly. "Why can't you just let them do what they need to do. It would just destroy the grandkids if you were to suddenly die."

"I'm not going to suddenly die," Duane assured them. "You all need to calm down and slow down. I might want a second opinion—there'd be nothing wrong with that, would there, Doctor?"

"Not a thing—I just wouldn't put off getting it, if I were you."

"You're not me, though—none of you are me," Duane said. "So please just all back off. There's a lot to think about here, and I intend to take my time thinking about it, okay?"

"It's not okay with me," Nellie said. "I think you should do it and do it now."

"Leave him alone," Dickie said. "He'll get around to it when he's ready."

"It's all Momma's fault," Julie cried. "If she hadn't run into that stupid milk truck she could have made Daddy eat good and he'd be healthy today."

"That's absurd," Nellie countered. "She never made Daddy eat anything healthy—how could she when she didn't even eat healthy herself?

"I've never seen Daddy eat a salad in my life," she added.

It seemed to Duane that a normal family argument was taking place, one not much different from countless other family arguments. Since he had no interest in participating in it, he began to walk away. Honor's office was only four blocks away, and he had a shrink appointment. He felt sure he could walk the four blocks, heart blockage or no heart blockage.

He was almost out the door when Julie noticed that he was leaving.

"Daddy you can't just go," she said.

"Yes, I can just go," he said. "I have an appointment with my psychiatrist—I think I need to tell her the big news. I'd like to know what she thinks about it."

"I hate her, we all hate her!" Julie burst out. "She's just some terrible old dyke—you're not crazy anyway, why do you have to go to a shrink?"

"Stop that dyke talk!" Nellie insisted. "I'm a dyke now, remember?"

"Yes, and I hate that too," Julie said. "Even if Zenas is kind of boring it would be better for the kids if you could just stay normal for a few more years instead of taking up with a little slut like Bessie."

"Don't call my girlfriend a slut!" Nellie yelled, shaking her fist in Julie's face.

Duane knew his family resented his attachment to Honor Carmichael. They might live in mansions in North Dallas, but, at heart, they were still Thalia girls—and in Thalia, for a family member to see a psychiatrist was still an embarrassment.

Lesbianism was an even worse admission.

"You two idiots shut up," Dickie said. "You're in a hospital. Behave yourselves."

"Fuck you, asshole!" Julie said. "All your wife does is sit home and smoke dope and watch soaps all day."

"At least she's not abandoning her children to go off and be a nun," Dickie said. Then he stalked off.

When the girls glared at one another, as they were glaring just then, they became the spitting image of their mother. No one could out-glare Karla, when her dander was up.

He turned to leave again, but Julie grabbed his arm.

"Daddy, you can't just walk off—you've got ninety percent blockage," Julie said.

"Well, that's just one doctor's opinion," Duane reminded her. "And even if it's true that leaves me ten percent blood flow. I think I can make it to Dr. Carmichael's on my ten percent."

"I hate her, I hate her, I hate her!" Julie said, loudly.

"Bye girls, thanks for coming," Duane said.

18

DUANE HAD NO TROUBLE walking the four shady blocks to Honor Carmichael's office—his arteries might be a ticking bomb within him but the fact didn't really affect his mood. It seemed good that his kids still fought with one another—at least they hadn't drifted so far apart that they had lost their sense of connection.

When he got to Honor's office, to his surprise he saw a black veil draped over the door handle—his first thought was that Jody Carmichael must have died. But when he went in and asked Honor's assistant, a lovely Hispanic girl, if that was the case she shook her head.

"Angie died, Mr. Moore," she said. "Dr. Carmichael has gone east with her ashes. They'll be scattering them today. Dr. Carmichael will be back tomorrow."

"That's a shock," he said. "I only met Angie once, but she didn't seem old."

"Smoking, probably. She died of lung cancer."

As Duane turned to go the assistant handed him a note. The note was in a heavy cream-colored envelope, with Honor's monogram on the back.

"She left this for you, in case you dropped by," the girl said.

Duane took the note. He felt reluctant to leave the cool offices, but he knew he must.

It surprised him that Honor had left the note—probably she was curious about his tests. He didn't open the note immediately. There was a Dairy Queen only half a mile down the street—he thought he might walk over, get a chocolate malt, and read his note.

As he was walking along he realized he had forgotten to retrieve his bike from Bobby Lee. Now that he was feeling almost himself again he wanted his bicycle. As he was strolling he called Bobby Lee on his cell and got him on the first ring.

"I need my bike," Duane said. "I'll meet you at the Dairy Queen on Holiday Street."

"Okay, but there's a small problem," Bobby said. "Your daughters have confiscated your bike."

"What? Who let them?"

"Hey, I only got one ball," Bobby Lee said. "I have to be careful around angry women, or I'll be out of business.

"Besides, to hear them tell it, you'll be on the operating table soon—how'd you escape?"

"On foot," Duane said. "And for your information I still have a will of my own. If you can find my bike steal it and bring it to me pronto. If you can't find it I guess I'll just buy a new one."

"Actually they didn't physically confiscate it," Bobby said. "It was more like a moral confiscation."

"Meaning they just told you not to let me have it?"

"Right."

"I'm glad you're able to grasp these subtle concepts—like moral confiscation. You haven't been going to night school on me, have you?"

"Nope, but you've been signing my paychecks for most of my life, whereas your daughters have never given me a dime."

"Oh, I see," Duane said. "You're a damn Marxist. Follow the money—is that it?"

"That's right about it," Bobby Lee said. "I'll be there in about twenty minutes if the Highway Patrol don't interfere. But keep in mind that it's still hot. If you was to keel over dead riding your bike around my ass would be grass."

"I don't plan to keel over, but I won't be pedaling around much in this heat, either," Duane assured him.

"I hope not, your daughters are mean," Bobby said.

Duane hung up and opened his note from Honor Carmichael. It was a short note—not to mention shocking.

Duane:
The oldest human wisdom is to fuck after a funeral. Be at home.
Honor

Duane was still holding the note in his hand when Bobby Lee showed up with his bicycle.

1 9

DUANE PUT HONOR'S NOTE back in the heavy cream envelope and stuck the envelope in his hip pocket. He didn't want Bobby Lee, or anyone, to know what the note said. Just having it on his person made him a little paranoid. Of course there was no way that Bobby lee could read a note that was in an envelope in his hip pocket—nobody could, and yet Duane still felt paranoid. The note promised to change everything—or did it?

Bobby Lee had just lifted Duane's bike out of the rear end of his pickup when Duane came out the door, took the bicycle, and put it right back in the rear of the pickup.

"I thought you wanted your bike," Bobby said. "Wasn't that why I just drove over here, risking the wrath of your daughters, I might add."

"Life is change, Bobby," Duane said. "The biking era just ended. The wheel has come full circle. What I need now is a pickup, one with good air-conditioning."

Bobby Lee jerked in surprise.

"*You* want a pickup—after all your vows and all these years?"

"I do, take me to the office," Duane said. "I'll have one of the secretaries lease me a pickup for a month or two."

On the way to the office Bobby Lee kept glancing at Duane—

but Duane, as near as he could tell, seemed to be breathing normally.

"If I was ever to go to a shrink what would be the first thing I ought to talk to her about?" he asked.

"How do you know it would be a her?"

"Well, yours is a her, and I like her looks," Bobby Lee said.

"If it's Honor or someone like her I'd jump right into the subject of your having just one ball."

"I might be too shy to mention a personal matter like that."

"Then what you'll probably do is go through life picking up girls at gas stations and watching them run off with hardened criminals—after you've married them, of course."

"I might overcome my shyness if the doctor looked kind," Bobby said. "Is Dr. Carmichael kind?"

"Yes, and she costs $190 an hour," Duane reminded him.

"I probably wouldn't need more than one or two sessions, stable as I am," Bobby Lee said. "If I was to need shock treatment or something I might have to put that part off till after I win the lottery."

Fortunately Julie and Nellie had gone back to Dallas. Nobody was there but three young secretaries.

"So is it tomorrow that you're having your operation, Mr. Moore?" one of the secretaries asked. "Nellie said they were hoping to get you in real soon."

"It's not going to be quite that quick," Duane told her. "What I do need, pronto, is a pickup I can lease."

Twenty minutes later—such being the power of the Moore name—a brand-new Toyota pickup arrived. The sight of it made Bobby Lee slightly jealous.

"That's what my pickup looked like twenty years ago," he observed.

"Bobby, there's no reason you can't buy yourself a new pickup oftener than every twenty years," Duane said. "You're not a pauper. In fact, before Anne Cameron came along you were our highest-paid employee. You were pulling in thousands and wasting most of it on worthless women."

"I suppose I *could* get a new pickup," Bobby allowed. "But why bother? It would look just like my old pickup after about three weeks."

"Good point."

Duane switched his bike from Bobby Lee's pickup to his spanking-clean new rental vehicle. Then he climbed in behind the wheel.

"Think you can still drive?" Bobby Lee asked. "Skills erode, you know. Use it or lose it, they say."

"Use it or lose it yourself," Duane said. "I can still drive."

And, to prove it, he drove away.

20

DUANE STOPPED OFF at Mike and Tommy's on his way to his cabin. Mike and Tommy exclaimed over his shiny white pickup, and Duane ate his fill of spring rolls and barbecued pork, the food he had been craving the day he had his heart attack.

Then he drove on to his cabin, which was stifling. He opened all the windows and did his best to air the place out. Then he took out Honor's note and read it again. The secretary had indicated that Honor would return sometime that day. She might already be in Wichita Falls—she might even be on her way to the cabin. His instructions were just to be at home, ready for sex. At least that was how he read the note. The note was the last of a number of strong shocks he had received lately: Julie's decision to become a nun, Nellie's gayness, Anne Cameron telling him he was weak with women, and, of course, his own collapse and discouraging angiogram.

About death, funerals, and fucking he knew Honor was right. The living needed to get life going again. But he had not expected Honor to want to get anything going with him. And was the cabin where she really expected him to be? What if by home she meant the big house? Honor and Angie Cohen had visited his famous garden once, but it was possible she didn't even know where the cabin was—and, even if she found it, it was not really a suitable place to receive a refined woman who was bent on seduction. The sheets hadn't been changed in a while, the floor was dusty, and the refrigerator empty except for a few beers.

Also, quite a few dead flies were stuck to the screen door.

Sweeping away the dead flies was about all Duane could do. Even as he swept he began to be sure that he was in the wrong place. Honor could have written the note in a low moment. She had given no previous sign of wanting him—but she *did* know that he was interested in her.

Also to be considered was the fact that women changed their minds. What seemed interesting one moment might seem bizarre the next.

He was in a hot place, with no amenities, waiting for a woman who might never come. On top of that, he had his own doubts. Did he really still want Honor? Was he really up to seeking love? More particularly, was he up for sex?

To none of those questions did he have a certain answer. He began to feel fretful and restless. A woman he had come to consider out of reach might be about to place herself in reach. In his fantasies he had imagined the two of them making love on a king-sized bed in a hotel. He had never once supposed she would come to his cabin. He felt uneasy; he began to hyperventilate. He told himself not to be silly—after all, Honor was just a human being who had had a recent grief. She was a doctor, not a goddess. He had no reason to fear her.

Mainly, he wished his sheets were cleaner—he wondered if he had time to race into Thalia, to the laundrymat. Then he remembered that the laundrymat was closed. There were many laundrymats in Wichita Falls that he might race to, but he fidgeted and stayed where he was.

While he was fretting he heard the sound of a car and looked across the plain to where the dirt road crossed the river. The car was a gray Volvo, Honor's car. It was weaving badly—once it even went briefly into the ditch but it pulled out and came on up his hill—soon it turned in at the cattle guard and wove its way to his cabin. Twice it veered and ran over small mesquite seedlings, but no harm was done. Duane supposed Honor might be crying—else why was she driving so erratically—but when he walked over to greet her he at once smelled gin on her breath. She opened the door, got out, and then stumbled straight into his arms.

"I'm drunk, don't kiss me," she said. She wore a T-shirt, white slacks, sandals. Sweat had formed a little puddle in the hollow of her throat, and the T-shirt was damp across her bosom.

"Whew," she said. "I really don't handle gin anymore."

"I'm surprised you found the cabin," Duane said. "This is not a main-traveled road."

"I was in your cabin twice," Honor said. "Just snooping. I even left clues, but I guess you're not that observant. I took it to mean you'd rather keep me as a fantasy—which is okay too."

Duane remembered that there had been a time or two when he had the sense that someone might have been in the cabin—he figured it was Nellie, a natural snoop like her mother. It had never occurred to him that it might have been Honor.

"I did notice but I figured it was one of my nosy daughters," he said.

Honor chuckled. Then she pulled off her sweaty T-shirt. Her breasts were heavier than he would have thought. She raised her arms and held them up, so he would notice the hair under her armpits.

"Anybody can grow a bush under their arms," she said. "Pull it—it's real."

Duane touched it, but didn't really pull it.

"You're a rather tentative seducer," Honor said. "Let's get out of the heat."

"We can get out of the sunlight but we can't get out of the

heat," he told her. "There's plenty of heat to be found inside the cabin."

"And soon to be more," she said. "Play by the rules now. Don't kiss me."

"I don't know what the rules are, but I'm sorry to hear about your friend," he said.

"No you're not, dummy," she said. She slipped a hand under his shirt and began to tease his nipples. Then she put her tongue in his ear, bit his earlobe lightly, then began to lick his eyelids.

"I'm very lingual," she said. "I don't intend to leave much of you unlicked."

Then she opened his shirt and put her mouth on his nipples.

When she stood up she wobbled so badly that Duane had to catch her.

"Whew, gin," she said. "Let's get on the bed."

"I meant to get those sheets washed," he said, apologetically.

Honor stared at him.

"Why would you suppose I care about the goddamn sheets?" she asked. "Why don't you just shut up and let this happen? Could you just pull my slacks off now?"

He did, rendering her naked.

"Why wear panties when you're only looking to fuck?" she asked. There was a trickle of sweat between her breasts.

"Here I am but don't put your mouth on me yet," she told him. "You might dip a finger in but give me the finger first."

Duane, uncertain, held out a finger—Honor pulled it into her mouth and wet it thoroughly.

"Saliva's a useful liquid," she said.

Duane felt his pants bulging, which Honor took note of. She sat up and opened his trousers, pushing them down his legs.

"Hello, Johnson," she said, pushing his trousers even farther down his legs, so she could cup his scrotum. Then she wet one of of her own fingers and slipped it under his scrotum to touch his asshole. The touch was so unexpected that Duane jumped.

"Ha, that always gets you country boys," Honor said.

As Honor continued to manipulate his dick and his balls Duane felt an orgasm coming.

"Stand up and take your pants off, silly," Honor said. Duane obeyed but Honor was still playing with him delicately.

"I'm getting there quick—too quick."

"Let her rip," she said. "I intend to keep you in bed all this day. You're perfectly welcome to get off first. I have a feeling you need to."

Then she briefly lowered her mouth to the head of his penis— she did this several times, never taking him very far in. Then she held his dick while he came copiously—to his shock he saw that his semen was rust-colored.

"Why do you look so alarmed, Duane?" she asked, not at all disconcerted by the rust-colored semen. She gave his dick a de-flating squeeze.

"It's never been red before," he said. "Does it mean I'm bleeding or something?"

Honor gave a husky laugh.

"Of course not," she said. "You are something of an ignoramus when it comes to sex, I'm afraid. Rusty semen just means you haven't been having sex often enough.

"You need to hook up with some little tootsie and fuck her brains out," she added.

"Why can't it be you?" he asked.

Honor chuckled.

"Let's see how the day goes, shall we?" she said.

21

SOME OF DUANE'S rust-colored semen had squirted on the bed-sheet—a little even got on Honor's leg. She swiped a little on her fingers, smelled it, and then put the finger in her mouth. Duane had seen such a thing done in porn movies but had never witnessed it with a real-life lover. Karla would never have been likely to eat his cum.

"There's an ice chest in the trunk of my car," Honor said. "I bought some liquor and some goodies—the keys are in my pants if you want to go get it."

When Duane came back with the ice chest Honor was sobbing. Tears streamed down her cheeks.

"I need the gin," she said. "I just lost the love of my life, after all," she said.

Duane opened the chest and handed her the gin, which she drank straight—three long swallows; then she set the bottle on the window by the bed. Duane wondered if this woman would have been interested in being naked with him if she hadn't been so drunk. Her body was slick with sweat—his too—and yet they hadn't begun to make love.

"I'm pretty amorous when I'm drunk," Honor said. "Want to watch me play with myself? Did your wife ever want you to watch her play with herself?"

"Karla—no, she didn't."

"Pity," Honor said. Then she wet two fingers and lowered them to her cunt.

"Wow, I'm pretty wet," she said. "I don't need the spit. Either I want you or gin makes me horny or both."

She reached for his hand and sucked on three of his fingers.

"Put them in me slow," she said, "and don't touch my clitoris."

Duane slipped his fingers inside her—easily, for she was pretty wet. She raised on her elbow. Duane had a kind of half erection. She reached over and cupped his balls again.

"I called Charlie Calvert and got the news on your angiogram," she said. "That means this is going to be a woman-superior fuck. I don't want you dying in the act, like Nelson Rockefeller did.

"Just lay back," Honor told him, and he obeyed. He felt embarrassed and nervous—he doubted that his erection was going to last. Honor was still playing with herself—she gave a heavy sigh, a pleased sigh. She took another long swallow of gin and straddled him.

"Relax, for God's sake," she said. "This isn't going to hurt."

Then she eased him into her, squeezing his cock to enlarge the erection.

Despite himself he came, when he had been inside her only half a minute. What would she think?

Honor rocked a little—he slipped out but she immediately reinserted him and rocked a little more—she held him in place with her muscles. Then she bent over and put her head on his chest. Cautiously, he put his arms around her. Again, she began to cry. The sheets were already as wet as if they had been hosed with water. Duane wanted to apologize for coming so quickly, but he held his peace. When Honor wanted talk she would talk.

"I didn't come here to trade orgasm for orgasm," she told him. "I came here to forget my loss and give you a little of what you want."

Duane slipped out of her, but Honor took no notice.

"There's a woman who's wanted me for twenty years," she

said, sitting up suddenly. "She's a painter, very famous. Angie hated her. And she may be one of the few women meaner than Angie. She lives on Long Island. I'm going to see her in about a month. I just like running with the high dykes, I guess."

Then she stepped out of bed. A trail of his semen was dripping down her thigh—it was a little less rusty-looking than the first load.

"I'm hungry, even if I'm drunk," she said. "Fortunately I brought goodies. Let's eat—then we'll get on with your belated sex education."

Besides the gin and a bottle of pepper vodka, the cooler contained caviar, foie gras, quail eggs, and cheese.

"Quail eggs?" he asked. "Where would you get quail eggs?"

"At a high-end deli," she said. "They go well at fancy brunches in the East—Evangeline Bruce always serves them."

Duane had no idea who Evangeline Bruce might be. He had only had red caviar before and was surprised at how good black caviar was. They sat at a little table, his little table, both still naked. Honor had a little mother-of-pearl spoon that she dipped the caviar with. A few of the black eggs dropped on her breasts.

"Want to lick 'em off?" she asked. "Regress for a moment. Lick a tit."

Duane's lick was so tentative that Honor looked dismayed.

"Good Lord," she said. "You don't know how to play at all, which means you had probably better stay away from Annie Cameron. She'll expect livelier action than this."

"I don't even know her," Duane. "I doubt she'd give me the time of day."

Honor ignored the comment. She wet two fingers and began to play with herself again, looking Duane full in the face as she did it.

"What's the most number of times you've come in one day?" she asked. With her other hand she swiped the black fish eggs off her breasts and ate them.

"I'd have to think."

"Then *think*, you idiot!" Honor said. "How many?"

"I think I remember three in one day when Karla and I were young," he said.

Honor smiled.

"You've already come twice with me," she reminded him. "We're going to break your record."

Duane was okay with that plan, and yet he felt a sadness creep in. The day would end and Honor Carmichael would drive away, probably forever. Whatever she taught him would be something he would never likely need to know again. At one point she put his dick between her breasts, then put it in her mouth and laved it for long stretches with her tongue. She straddled him several more times, rocking very gently. Once she lay beside him, a leg over his body, so she could guide him in and out, or at least as far out as his half erection would go. She coaxed more orgasms out of him: his semen became whitish again. Once she let him stroke the sheath that hid her clitoris. She made him enter her doggy fashion—again he had a hard time staying hard.

"I mostly draw the line at anal sex now," she said. "Once Angie hurt me with a dildo—a big dildo. I suppose I'm a masochist, but I'm not *that* much of a masochist. I told her not to put that big ugly thing in me, but she did it anyway."

All day, sweat poured off both of them.

As the sun set they finished off the caviar, the foie gras, the quail eggs, the cheeses, and most of the vodka.

"When it gets dark I'm going to suck you off one more time—then I'm out of here," Honor said. "It's been a long time since I've fucked all day. I think I got you off six times, although the well was pretty close to dry that last time.

"Despite what you might think, it felt good," she said. Duane could not swear that she had had even one orgasm.

"It helped me," she said, as she was getting into her car. "I'm not your doctor anymore—I'm just your friend."

Then she left. It saddened Duane that they had never kissed.

22

THE NEXT MORNING Duane felt apathetic. He got up but didn't bother making coffee. He remembered that once a year or so ago he had such a terrible anxiety attack that he could only control it by taking baths—several baths, very hot. In the course of that day he had used up all the towels in the cabin. Karla came by in the afternoon and saw the towels, which convinced her that Duane had been indulging in an all-day fuck, as she put it, with some woman she didn't know about.

Now he really had enjoyed pretty much an all-day fuck with Honor Carmichael, and the room not only looked like it, it smelled like it. If Karla had stepped into the cabin just then her bloodhound nose would have instantly detected the truth.

Duane stripped the bed and threw the dirty sheets and towels into the back of his pickup, meaning to take them to Wichita Falls and launder them himself. He kept replaying his day with Honor in his mind and concluded that he was woefully out of practice as a lover. Honor had led and he had merely followed orders, to the best of his ability. Whether she had an orgasm or not, she seemed to have enjoyed herself. For her it had been all play; for him it was mostly worry. He felt that Honor would have wanted to be woman-superior whether his arteries had been blocked or not.

Some of the things she said to him, without turning a hair, would have turned the hair of any woman he had ever been involved with, including Karla, who liked to think she called a spade a spade.

"In my straight years I never liked plain fucking very much, but I always liked giving head," she said, before taking his dick in her mouth again.

Then there were the darker revelations—Angie Cohen and the dildo, for example. Why would Honor allow it? And yet the picture of her being anally penetrated by a big dildo wouldn't entirely leave his mind.

In the afternoon he drove into Wichita Falls and did his laundry. He went to his office and picked up a few phone messages, one of which was from Honor's receptionist. What the message said was that Dr. Carmichael was terminating her practice, effective immediately. All patients were referred to Dr. David Morgan, who would attend to prescription refills and the like.

There was a beep, and that was that. Honor was gone, leaving him with a fine but confusing memory. It still bothered him that they had never kissed. On the way home he stopped at a supermarket and filled the whole rear of his pickup with groceries. He bought lots of frozen food and lots of liquor. He bought everything that he might need if he decided to withdraw even farther than he had already withdrawn. He might sit on his hill for a month or more. If he did that, slowly, eventually, he would begin to forget Honor Carmichael. She had enriched his life immensely, but now she had left his life. He knew that he couldn't will her out of his thoughts, but gradually, if he were patient, his thoughts would find a way around her. A month might do it, so he provisioned for a month. If he got tired of frozen pizza he could always drive his new pickup over to Mike and Tommy's and eat a few spring rolls or some barbecued pork.

23

THREE DAYS after retreating to the grocery-filled cabin, Duane saw a dust cloud of unusual magnitude filling the air above the road. It was Bobby Lee, he imagined, but the old Toyota pickup Bobby Lee nursed along wouldn't make a dust cloud of that magnitude. It must mean that Bobby had bought a new pickup with oversized wheels—which proved to be the case.

"New wheels," Duane remarked, when Bobby Lee braked his new red pickup to a stop.

"Have you taken Miss Cameron for a ride in it yet?" he added.

"No—that snooty bitch is the bane of my existence," Bobby Lee said. "You ought not to have inflicted her on me at this stage of my life."

"I didn't inflict her, Dickie did," Duane reminded him. "Anyway she'll be gone to Indonesia in a few months—you'll just have to tough it out till then."

"You got a FedEx from your doctor," Bobby Lee told him. "I rescued it from Annie. I think she was about to trash it."

Duane took the envelope, supposing it was from Dr. Peppard—there was still the matter of the clogged arteries to think about. Duane was doing nothing, other than a lot of staring into space, the matter of the arteries didn't feel urgent—not to him, anyway. Of course it felt urgent to his daughters, who called him frequently—so often that he finally turned his cell phone off.

The FedEx, though, was from Honor, and it didn't just contain a letter. It contained plane tickets from DFW to Boston, a hotel reservation at the Ritz-Carlton, and a sheet of information from Massachusetts General Hospital, where he was set to see a cardiologist named Thomas Higginson, who would do another angiogram and other tests as needed. There was a short letter from Honor, written in her firm hand:

Duane:

Mass General is the best diagnostic hospital in America, and Tommy Higginson and I are old friends. Please submit to whatever tests he says you need. My niece Cherry will meet your plane, take you to the hotel, then the hospital, and back to the airport. I'll be in Europe a few weeks—don't balk on me. We need to know what's what about your heart.

Your physical heart, that is.

I'll be in Texas the week you get home. You'll hear from me.

Honor

P.S. I enjoyed our day of sex perhaps more than you realized. You've got a lot of loosening up to do. Maybe I can help.

"Good news?" Bobby Lee asked.

"Well, news," Duane said. "I guess I'm going to Boston to get tested."

Bobby Lee looked uncomfortable—he took off his dozer cap and put it back on. He was looking into the distance—the same distance Duane often stared into.

"What's the matter?"

"Bad arteries ain't the only kind of problem a person can have," Bobby Lee reminded him. "For example, an old friend and family employee could find himself in the middle of a family dispute that's no business of his to even know about."

"What in hell does that mean?"

"It means your daughters are both dead set against your going to Boston—they want you to have the tests done in Dallas."

"Wait a minute," Duane insisted. "I just found out ten seconds ago that Honor wanted me to go to Boston for the tests. How would my daughters know anything about it?"

"Good question, Sherlock," Bobby Lee. "Somebody might have found out by reading your e-mail—that's one possibility."

Duane realized that was the likely explanation. Lots of e-mails flowed through his office—he only bothered to collect them every week or so.

Duane began to get an annoyed feeling. The FedEx envelope had been open when Bobby handed it to him, and Honor's envelope had not been sealed.

"Who do you think might have read my e-mail?" he asked.

Bobby shrugged. "Miss Nipples has been to Dallas twice lately—she and your girls are best buddies, now, you know."

"I didn't know. Been to Dallas to do what?"

Bobby shrugged again.

"I wasn't invited, so how would I know?" he said. "I suppose they eat fancy food and go dancing. Probably they spend a lot of time cussing your shrink."

"I wish Dickie had never hired that girl," he said. He was feeling more annoyed by the minute.

"Dickie likes money a lot more than you ever did," Bobby Lee said. "I could always get you to go fishing now and then. Hell, we even went to Ruidoso to the horse races quite a few times. Dickie don't fish and I doubt he's ever given a thought to the ponies. He used to spend all his time taking drugs, and now he spends all his time making money."

"I'm glad you mentioned the horse races," Duane said.

"Maybe we ought to go out and watch the ponies for a couple of weeks. That way I wouldn't have to fight with my girls over Boston or whatever."

Bobby Lee looked distressed.

"I'd love to but I can't," he said. "Jessica's home."

"Uh-oh. Is that good or bad?"

"Enjoy the races," Bobby Lee said.

24

DUANE THOUGHT his decision to spend a couple of weeks at the horse races in New Mexico was a good one. He could just get in his new pickup and go. Nobody need be worried and perhaps the argument about where his heart tests were to take place might never happen.

He didn't want a discussion to happen, since it would only boil down to another chance for his daughters to attack Honor Carmichael. Running off seemed the best solution—besides, he *did* like to watch the ponies run.

Somehow, though, this smart plan never got put into action. Once he even packed his backpack—the same one he had taken to Egypt—but he didn't leave. It was easier just to sit on his hill and pay an occasional visit to Mike and Tommy at the Asia Wonder Deli. Once he took his rod and walked over to the nearby stock tank to fish. He only caught perch, and he threw them back, but it was something to do.

It wasn't that he expected Honor to show up and have sweaty sex with him anytime soon. He didn't expect anybody to show up, and, except for Bobby Lee, few did. He went to his office in Wichita Falls once in a while, but he did not go to Thalia. He didn't want to be in Thalia—not for a while, at least.

Once, remembering his day of sex with Honor, he found he had an erection—a rare erection. So he masturbated and, afterward, felt sad. What he had just done, at his age, represented a kind of sexual defeat.

Sometimes he spent a whole day just looking off his hill. The great emptiness to the northwest seemed to equalize the emptiness inside him. August ended and September began. Dove season opened—he could hear the pop of shotguns from the fields and pastures around him. He phoned Bobby Lee and asked him to drop off a shotgun and a box of shells, which Bobby Lee did. His old friend had a black eye. Bobby Lee didn't mention it and Duane didn't inquire.

Duane spent a week of almost total silence, during which the only people he saw were roughnecks or cowboys passing on the road. One afternoon he walked down to the tank and shot three doves with three shots. He dressed the birds, wrapped them in bacon, and broiled them. They were excellent, and yet he did no more hunting. Instead of eating dove every night he ate Fritos and bean dip, or a pizza, or a peanut butter sandwich, or spring rolls from Mike and Tommy's. He forgot about Ruidoso and the horses. He spent more and more time doing less and less.

Then, a week before he was to fly off to Boston, his daughters came, bringing Anne Cameron with them.

25

"WE'RE YOUR *FAMILY*, Daddy—don't you think we have your best interests at heart?" Nellie asked, loudly.

It was still hot in the cabin—he offered the three of them beers, which they accepted, and they all walked over to a big tree, a sycamore, whose shade Duane used as a kind of patio. He had cut a number of mesquite stumps to serve as chairs. Nelly and Julie each sat on a stump, but Anne Cameron just crossed her long legs and sat on the ground. Duane made do with a stump.

"Sure, honey," he said. "I know you both have my best interests at heart." He was making every effort to be friendly and pleasant.

"Then why are you going to let that woman drag you off to that old Yankee hospital?" Julie asked. "We've got perfectly good hospitals right here in Dallas."

"What's Yankee got to do with it?" Duane asked. "The Civil War's been over a long time. Boston's just as much part of America as Dallas—I've always heard it's a good town."

"It's a *great* town—went to school there," Anne Cameron said. "I love Boston."

Nellie whirled on her indignantly.

"Whose side are you on, Annie?" she asked. "We don't *want*

him to go to Boston. That's the whole point of this visit—to talk him out of it."

"I know that," Annie said calmly. "That's your desire and, if you'll remember, I advised you not to bother."

"Well, we happen to *want* to bother!" Julie said.

Annie looked at Duane and shrugged.

Duane decided he might as well stir the pot a little. Right at the moment he was not feeling pleased with his daughters. They wore too much makeup, had on too much jewelry, and both had their jaws set in the way that he had always disliked in their mother. Karla enjoyed pushing people around. She never relented, and seldom forgave those, like himself, who just ignored her orders, her wishes and her rage.

Both his daughters now looked just as their mother had looked when somebody crossed her.

"We don't like it that you'd rather do what some old dyke wants you to than to listen to your own daughters who love you."

"Nellie, I don't want to hear any more of that," Duane said. "Don't be calling Dr. Carmichael names—seems like it wasn't so long ago that you were gay yourself. Am I right?"

Anne Cameron smiled to herself.

"No, she's normal again—Bessie ran off with a barrel racer," Julie said. Another bad trait of his daughters was their tendency to gloat over one another's romantic disasters—of which there had been plenty over the years.

"Momma hated that woman! Hated her!" Nellie said. "Why won't you even be loyal to Momma's memory?"

"Your mother was the jealous type," Duane said. "She managed to find something to hate about every woman I was ever friendly with. I don't care what she thought of my doctor—nor what you think about her either. She's an MD and she knows a lot about hospitals. I have a serious heart condition. I want the best doctor I can find to advise me about it—and if Dr. Carmichael thinks Mass General is the place to go then I have every intention of taking her advice."

There was a silence. Anne Cameron seemed to be thinking her own thoughts.

"Can't you say something, Annie?" Julie asked. "Can't you make him see that he's making a fool of himself with that old hag?"

"I suppose I could try to get him to let me set him up at UCLA—that's a good hospital too. But I don't think he's likely to change his plans, and he's right to look farther than Dallas. I wouldn't get a hangnail treated in Dallas, much less anything serious."

Both the sisters looked at her in shock.

"You said you were on our side—you said you hated her too," Julie managed.

"No, now you're confused," Anne said. "What I said was that my aunt Linda hated Angie Cohen. My family's very anti-Semitic. My father resigned from the yacht club the day they admitted their first Jew.

"I don't think anyone in my family really knew Dr. Carmichael," she went on. "They just assumed that if she was living with Angie Cohen then she must be bad."

"The girls wouldn't know about anti-Semitism," Duane said. "There's not been a single Jew living in Thalia in my lifetime."

"No, but there's plenty of the greedy fuckers living in North Dallas," Nellie said.

"Look," Duane said. "You don't seem to know it but Dr. Carmichael has closed her practice in Wichita Falls. She's in Europe. I don't know that I'll ever see her again, but I hope I see her again because without her help last year I'd probably be dead. I understand that you don't want me to replace your mother with another woman—that' s normal enough."

"Oh, we don't care if you have a girlfriend, Daddy," Julie said.

"We just want it to be someone from our part of the country, not some Yankee dyke."

Duane stood up.

"Honor Carmichael was born and raised in Vernon—not even fifty miles from here," he said.

"I don't care where she was born—she's not like us," Julie cried.

"Well, that's true—she's not like you," Duane said. "But it might be that you'd be happier women if you were more like her."

"Whoa!" Annie Cameron said, suppressing a giggle.

"Shut up, you're a fucking snob yourself," Nellie cried.

Duane felt a sadness—he had thought he and Karla had done a good job of raising their daughters—but now he wasn't so sure.

"I'm not a snob," Annie Cameron said. "I work in a dingy little office. But I *am* educated, and you two aren't."

"You said you'd help us but you didn't, didn't!" Julie said, bitterly.

"Say not the struggle naught availeth," Annie said.

"What the fuck does that mean?" Nellie asked.

"It means I might help you yet—I'm thinking of a plan," Annie said, with a girlish grin.

"A plan—what fucking plan?" Julie asked.

"I'm getting tired of hearing the F-word from you two," Duane put in.

"Didn't I tell you that the hospital where he means to do the tests is a great hospital?" Annie said. "Dr. Carmichael was right to send him there. He'll be gone two days—big deal. It's how he spends the rest of his life that you two really ought to be thinking about."

"Well, he's not spending it with *her!*" Julie declared.

"What if I got him to spend it with me—would you like that any better?" Annie said quietly.

"I once thought you were our friend," Nellie said. "I thought you'd help us. But now I think you're just a snobby little cunt from California."

"You were just pretending to be like us," Julie said. "You're not really like us at all."

"What do you think, Boss Man?" Annie asked.

"I'm going to Boston to get my tests," Duane said. "That's as far as my thinking will take me right now."

"And you'll see *her*, won't you?" Julie said.

"Nope," he said. "Dr. Carmichael is in Europe and I think she means to stay there for a while. I'm going to get some tests done in a good hospital, that's all."

"It's not all—it's just the beginning of us losing you!" Nellie said. "We've been losing you more and more ever since you parked your pickup and started that stupid walking. Everyone in town thinks you did it because we drove you crazy taking drugs and having wild boyfriends. Not only did you embarrass us by walking everywhere, you had to start seeing a psychiatrist too. Now everyone thinks we've got mental illness in our family."

"Honey, what the people in Thalia think doesn't really matter," Duane said—he was still determined to be calm and reasonable. "None of us live in Thalia anymore. I think myself that I'd be a happier man today if I'd moved out of Thalia fifteen years ago."

"Whoa!" Annie Cameron said again.

"Stop saying 'Whoa!' What do you think we are, horses?" Nellie said.

"In this context 'whoa' is merely a term of astonishment," Annie said. She had remained cool and unruffled throughout the conversation. She had remained courteous—an ability Duane admired.

Unfortunately neither of his daughters seemed to care about courtesy. Their mother hadn't cared that much for it, either; it saddened him to realize that he'd raised an unmannerly brood of mostly spoiled children.

Julie was determined to make one last try.

"Look, Nellie and I have two big mansions mostly going to waste," she said. "If you'd just have your tests done in Dallas you could stay with us and be waited on hand and foot."

Duane just shook his head.

"I like waiting on myself—that's why I live alone," Duane said.

Both girls began to cry again.

"You're not giving us a chance, Daddy!" Nellie cried. "You're just not giving us a chance!"

"No, I'm giving my heart a chance," Duane said. "I'm giving it a chance by taking it to a really good hospital."

The girls gave up and went back into the cabin to use the bathroom. Anne Cameron got up, walked over to Duane, and stood on tiptoe, as if she meant to whisper something in his ear. Instead she bit his earlobe lightly. It startled Duane hugely—he jumped back, remembering as he did that Honor Carmichael had stuck her tongue in his ear before going on to more serious caresses.

"Penny for your thoughts, Mr. Boss Man," Annie said, smiling.

Duane had set himself to resist Annie Cameron—even to dislike her—but now that she was beside him his resistance wouldn't hold. She seemed eager to make mischief of some kind, between him and his daughters or him and Honor; hers seemed to be likable mischief, with no real malice in it. He couldn't dislike her. One minute she was demure, the next minute she was biting his earlobe.

"I won't kiss anybody who chews tobacco," Annie said. "Sort of limits my romantic life here in Copenhagen country, Mr. Moore."

"I've never chewed," Duane told her.

"Then we should get rid of your girls and fuck like snakes," Annie said. "You can decide for yourself the great question of whether young pussy is better than old pussy. Want some chewing gum?"

Duane took the chewing gum.

"Whatever we do, or don't do, I don't think we need to let my daughters know we're doing it or not doing it."

"Oh sure," Annie said. "Let 'em be mad at you about Honor Carmichael. They don't need to be mad at you about me—or mad at me about you. They are *your* children—better to keep the peace as best we can."

She took a pen out of his pocket and wrote an address and phone number on the back of his checkbook.

"My apartment," she said. "I'll ride back to Thalia with the girls and meet you in Wichita Falls in about an hour and a half. I grew up in Tiburon, California, where it's cool. I'm afraid I'd pass out in no time in that cabin of yours. You don't really have some big objection to air-conditioning, do you?"

Duane shook his head. His daughters were just coming out of the cabin, fanning themselves.

"Don't take every word I say seriously," Annie said. "I talk wilder than I actually am. I'll bring some shrimp and cottage cheese and tomatoes. We don't really have to fuck like snakes. We can just eat shrimp salad and get to know one another a little, if you'd like to."

"I'd like to," Duane said.

26

ANNIE CAMERON'S "PAD," as she liked to call it, was an apartment in a nice part of town, near the country club. Karla had several times tried to get Duane to move to that very part of town, but he could not be persuaded. Now, driving in the early dusk, he smiled at the thought of how mad Karla would be if she knew he was driving to that very part of town to see a young woman her son had hired—a young woman who casually let her nipples show when at work. Though Karla had been dead two years, he could imagine her outrage vividly.

Driving into town to meet Annie, Duane found himself pondering what, if anything, he owed Honor Carmichael. Their day of sex left him more in love with Honor than ever—but it had clearly not been the same with her. She wasn't in love with him at all, and didn't pretend to be. She had more or less let him know that she would probably take the woman painter as a lover pretty soon. Perhaps she would discover that she wanted a little more time with him—but probably not much more time. Also she had suggested that he needed to loosen up and find more sex. Plainly, in her opinion, he needed practice.

Annie Cameron had seemed to offer a sexual opening when she suggested that they get together and fuck like snakes, but then she had immediately retreated from that statement. She had bitten his ear, of course, but that was probably just showing off.

So he was at sea, really. He loved Honor Carmichael and he was unable to dislike Annie Cameron, the tall, playful girl from Tiburon, California.

Anne's apartment was on the second floor of a posh—for Wichita Falls—apartment complex. As he walked past her window he smelled shrimp grilling. Anne opened the door before he rang the bell; she was dressed demurely in a white shirt and slacks. She was wearing a bra—he could see the straps—and had tucked up her hair. She looked like a nervous teenager.

"I guess this is the moment of truth," she said. "I'm about to let a man into my apartment. I haven't, you know, since I arrived a month ago—you'll be the very first male to cross my threshold."

"Because of the chewing tobacco, I expect," Duane said lightly.

"No, it's because I'm scared of men—particularly of large uneducated men."

Duane smelled bourbon on her breath. There was a candle at the little kitchen table—when Annie reached to light it her hand shook.

"I'm extremely nervous," she admitted, not looking at him. "If you'll just hold steady I might settle down."

"Maybe if I had a drink of whatever you're drinking we'd both feel a little steadier," Duane said. "Those shrimp smell good."

"They are good," she said. "I hope you don't mind Thai noodles. It's interesting that I don't feel scared of you."

"Why would you be?"

"Because mostly I'm scared of men," she said. "Bourbon with ice or bourbon straight?"

"I'll get it," Duane said. "You've got those noodles to think of." He felt a sense of relief. The evening had seemed as if it might involve a sexual challenge, but it was already clear that that was unlikely. Annie Cameron was like a gawky teenager, who was nervous at the thought of making dinner for her parents—or maybe for her boyfriend's parents. It had been a long time since anyone had been nervous about making dinner for him.

There was almost no furniture in the apartment—a long couch, a futon, a desk with a computer on it, a small table, a flat-screen TV, and two chairs.

"I know, it's minimalist—but it's okay for a six months stay," Annie said. "Do you think you could subtract from our relation-ship every single word or gesture that I've said or made to you that might be considered a sexual invitation?"

Duane smiled. "You mean you didn't mean it when you bit my ear?" he said, taking a warming swallow of bourbon.

"No, and I didn't mean it when I said we should fuck like snakes, either," she said. "Besides which it was a lie the day I met you when I told you my nipples got hard because I was thinking about my sexy boyfriend, Ruel. I never had a boyfriend named Ruel—my nipples just got hard because of the office air-conditioning. The fact is I haven't had much sexual experience."

She scooped the grilled shrimp onto a plate and put it on the table.

"I feel compelled to act as if I were hot to trot, but in fact I'm not hot to trot. I never let my boyfriends shave my legs or do any-thing like that. The only thing I'm really good at is geology. I may be a dud in bed but I can really find out what's under the rocks.

"But enough about me, let's eat," she said, slicing a couple of fresh tomatoes. She put a steaming bowl of Thai noodles on the table and set out a couple of sauces for the shrimp.

The food was delicious. Duane was awkward with chopsticks, which was all that had been provided. His awkwardness was so obvious that at one point Annie leaned across the table and guided his hand until he got the hang of it. She didn't meet his eye, but she was clearly relieved that he liked her food. And Duane really *did* like it. His eating had been erratic lately—it was nice to be offered delicious food that he didn't have to cook himself.

The cook, though, was in a low mood. She had three drinks—Duane had two.

"I suppose most of us try to pretend that we feel sexier than we do," Duane told her. "It's no big sin. I kind of thought you were just play-acting anyway."

Annie looked at him thoughtfully, but she didn't smile.

"Did it make you think I might be fun to fuck?" she asked.

Duane nodded.

"I'm not really fun to fuck, though," she said. "The Copenhagen cowboys don't want to hear that. They're *sure* I'm fun to fuck. But I won't kiss them or fuck them either. Let 'em burn, I say."

"I expect you'll be glad to get to Indonesia," he said. "You can eat food like this every night."

"Yes, but otherwise it won't be very different," Annie said. "Lots of men will want me and I won't want them at all. The only difference is that they'll be chewing betel nut, not Copenhagen."

She looked bleak. Duane got up, took his plate to the sink, and put an arm around Annie Cameron's shoulder. She took his hand and held it gratefully.

"That's a really comfortable couch," she said. "I bet it's more comfortable than the bed in your cabin. You would be doing me a huge favor if you'd sleep on it tonight—chastely, I mean."

"Okay, fine," he said. "It's pretty sultry out at my old cabin. Most nights I end up sleeping outside."

He wondered if she would explain why she wanted him to sleep on the couch—but she didn't. She disappeared into her bathroom and emerged in a bathrobe and old flannel pajamas.

"I haven't had a good night's sleep since I got here," she said. "I'm too scared of being raped. These apartments have such flimsy doors. Some big linebacker type could bust right in and catch me.

I've rejected dozens of them. I guess I just worry that one of them will get mad enough or drunk enough to come after me."

"Have a good sleep," Duane said.

The couch was indeed very comfortable. The two drinks had relaxed him and yet he didn't sleep for a while. He heard Annie Cameron thrashing around on the futon. At some point she turned on her little radio, very low.

At five in the morning, just as the light was coming, Annie eased down on the couch beside him.

"Could you just hold me, Mr. Moore? I've been having real bad dreams."

Duane held her as requested. Very soon her breathing evened out and she slept. Duane held her for a couple of hours—mainly she smelled young, as his daughters had once smelled young. Annie made, from time to time, little shiftings and adjustments in her position. The couch was spacious, there was plenty of room, but Annie's movements were tropic—she wanted her body as close to his as possible. At one point he had to turn himself to conceal from her that he had an erection. The last thing he wanted was to scare her, sexually.

When she finally awoke, about seven, she lay in his arms and looked blank, as children do when they haven't quite got their sleep out.

"My goodness, Mr. Moore, thank you," she said. "That's the best sleep I've had for months." Her voice was the voice of a sleepy teenager.

"Thank you so much—I mean *so* much!" she said. Then she squeezed his hand.

"You're welcome," Duane said.

27

"WANT SOME EGGS PROVENÇALE, Mr. Moore?" Annie asked—she was fully awake but had not moved from his side on the couch. Her pajama shirt had hiked up a little, exposing her belly button. She seemed to trust Duane completely, as a child trusts.

"I might if I knew what they were," he said.

"They're just eggs, with some tomatoes and garlic, or maybe some herbs," she said, jumping up suddenly.

"You don't have to call me Mr. Moore," he told her. She was already cracking eggs into a skillet.

"You could just call me Duane—everybody else does," he said.

Annie looked at him gravely and shook her head.

"You may call me Annie, but I want to call you Mr. Moore," she said. "I don't quite know why—I think it just sounds more respectful. And, on the PR front, it'll help a little when people find out we're living together."

The remark startled Duane. Was he now living with Annie Cameron—after all, it had just been one night.

"I know—just one night," she said. "But you liked staying with me, didn't you?"

She was squeezing oranges.

"I sure did," he said.

It earned him a delightful smile.

113

"And I liked having you—whole wheat toast okay?"

He nodded.

"Don't you think you've kind of worn out your recluse-in-a-cabin thing?" she asked, serving him some orange juice.

Eggs Provençale with whole wheat toast followed shortly. The breakfast was as tasty as the dinner had been.

"You eat, it's my time to run—I usually do three miles," she said.

A minute later, in running garb, she slipped out, returning twenty-odd minutes later dripping sweat. She went straight to the shower, emerging in her work clothes: cutoffs and a plain man's shirt. She dumped bananas, strawberries, apples, and grains into a blender and made herself a smoothie. Then she sat at the table with Duane and sucked down the smoothie, leaving a little strawberry ring on her upper lip.

Duane felt at ease, happy just to sit and look at Annie.

"When's Boston?" she asked.

"One week from today."

Annie looked at a thoroughly marked up calendar on her refrigerator door.

"I'd go with you and look after you but Dickie said I have to be in San Angelo that week—we're trying to tie together a big lease."

"I'll be fine in Boston, I expect," Duane said.

"I know," she said. "You'll be fine. But I want to be helpful. Why don't you move in for a week? I could feed you really good food—sort of build you up for your trip."

She looked momentarily nervous, as if fearful that he would turn down her invitation, but he had no intention of turning it down. He felt quite comfortable with Annie and she was mostly comfortable with him. Why not move in?

"That's fine—all I have to move are my toiletries and maybe a change of clothes."

Annie stopped fretting and looked at him—there was relief in her look.

"You mean you'll just do it?" she asked.

"Yep," he said. "I like being here. I like you. Why wouldn't I stay?"

"That's so great!" she said. "If it wasn't against the rules I'd kiss you."

Duane didn't say a word, but he found himself hoping that one day kissing wouldn't be against the rules.

28

THAT NIGHT Annie served him grilled halibut and English peas, plus tomatoes, of course, and a salad. Duane had spent the day relaxing in her apartment. Rather than drive out to his cabin to collect his toiletries, he bought new toiletries at a Circle K. In the afternoon his spirits slipped a bit. He wondered if Annie might just be passing through an insecure phase. Once she got through it she might not want an old man taking up space in her apartment. Besides that she was due to leave in five months—he could already sense how much he would miss her.

But when Annie came skipping in with their meal his spirits rose at once. The gossip from Thalia was that Jessica had thrown a hammer at Bobby Lee—the hammer missed Bobby but hit his bird dog, Cotton, who now traveled with a limp. Duane felt very happy as he watched Annie prepare their meal. Perhaps she felt happy too, because she kept looking at him and smiling. In relief—if that was what it was—they both drank too much bourbon. In trying to help her wash up Duane stumbled and broke a dish.

"Mr. Moore, you could just let me do this," Annie said lightly, though she took the broken dish in stride. For a time they merely sat together, both tipsy, on the couch.

Then Annie disappeared and emerged ready for bed. Again she wore flannel pajamas and an old bathrobe.

Again, she thrashed on the futon, while Duane dozed on the couch. At four A.M. Annie stumbled to the couch.

"Bad dream," she mumbled.

"I'll hold you," Duane said.

He held her—at one point she threw a leg over him, as a teenager might. She slept with her mouth open—he could see her teeth. At one point she gasped. Then she said "don't." He didn't think the word was meant for him.

Again, when she awakened, she looked blank for several minutes.

"I've never slept this deeply before," she told him. "I got us lox for breakfast."

Then she went back to sleep.

29

"IT'S LIKE I'm a split personality, Mr. Moore," Annie said. "In my work I'm totally organized and competent—but in my life I'm not."

She had come out of the shower with a towel around her head, topless, in jeans, nervous because she was apt to be late for work. Duane was washing up after their lox and bagels. Annie was all legs and shoulders, small-breasted, and in a hurry. When she stepped into the kitchen area to take a quick sip of espresso, one of her breasts brushed his arm—she didn't notice, but he did.

"It's this goddamn air-conditioning," she said. "It's too cold and it makes my nipples perk up. Then guys wander in and make the mistake of thinking that it's them I'm interested in, which is not the case."

She spotted a bra in a pile of laundry, put the bra on, put her shirt on, grabbed the black bag with her laptop in it, and started for the door. But then she whirled, came back to the kitchen, and gave him a hug.

"Don't break all my dishes," she said, and left. Duane went to the window and watched her slip into the Lexus—just before she closed the door she looked up at him, waved, and gave him another dazzling smile. It was as if she knew he would look at her at just that moment. She had counted on it. Unconfident as she was in many ways, she wasn't unconfident of her appeal to him.

Later, feeling a little restless, Duane drove over to Mike and Tommy's for lunch. Bobby Lee's new pickup with the oversized tires was parked there when he drove up.

"Where have *you* been?" Bobby Lee inquired, when Duane walked in. "I've been out to the cabin two nights in a row to see if you wanted to help me lay a trotline but you wasn't there. And you wasn't in town, either."

"I was in town, but not the town you were thinking of," Duane admitted. "It got too sultry in the cabin. Annie's been letting me sleep on her couch—just till it cools off a little."

He knew he was releasing big news into the gossip stream—but Bobby Lee, who had a three-day stubble and a haggard look, didn't seem at all surprised.

"Join the club," Bobby said. "We're in the same boat. Jessica lets me sleep on *our* couch. There's no sex and damn little cooking."

"Then I'm better off than you," Duane said. "Annie's just a roommate but there's excellent cooking."

Duane started to warn Bobby Lee not to mention what he had just told him, but after looking closely at his old friend he decided the warning wasn't necessary.

"You look like hell," he said. "Maybe you ought to get counseling."

"I went wrong at birth, which means it would be too long a story," Bobby Lee said.

"I might help you with the trotline, if you still want to," Duane said—it was more than evident that Bobby needed a little cheering up.

"Annie started wearing a bra to work," Bobby said. "I suppose that's due to the influence of Uncle Duane."

"It's the air-conditioning's influence," Duane said. "It wasn't our charm that made her titties poke up."

"Damn," Bobby Lee said. "I wish my wife would run away again."

"There's something called divorce."

Bobby just sighed.

"If I file for divorce she might get my new pickup," he said. "I couldn't bear to lose my new pickup—it's the one thing I got that boosts my self-esteem."

"I see," Duane said.

"I doubt you do," Bobby told him.

30

ANNIE HAD ASKED Duane to buy a flank steak and marinate it a few hours in a marinade she liked. Duane knew a butcher he trusted—he easily secured the steak and even got a bunch of sweetbreads for good measure. Then he stopped at his office to see if he had accumulated any messages. He asked about Dickie, who was in Chicago. Duane was about to leave when one of the young secretaries handed him a fresh e-mail. It was Honor:

Duane:
I'm coming back from France a little early. I'll be in Boston in the late afternoon of the day you're being tested. Maybe we can have dinner. I'll check at the hotel.
Honor

Duane felt happier. Boston was not a city he was familiar with. Having Honor there would be wonderful. Besides, she could help him understand the results of his tests, if they were available that soon.

He went home and marinated the flank steak—the sweetbreads he kept apart until he talked to Annie about them. Not everybody liked sweetbreads.

He kept the e-mail in his hip pocket. Not everybody liked Honor Carmichael, either. He thought about concealing the e-mail, which, after all, was really only his business. But Annie posed a different problem. He wanted to win her trust. If he concealed the e-mail and she found out about it from one of the secretaries, she would undoubtedly be upset and he might never win her trust. He was enchanted with Annie and didn't want to ruin what they had.

So he put the e-mail on the counter, where Annie would see it when she waltzed in, and she did waltz in at the usual hour. Her eye fell on the e-mail immediately. Duane was stretched out on the couch, watching CNN.

Annie arched her graceful neck slightly, as a thoroughbred filly might if a badger had suddenly appeared in her path. She had a big bag of groceries on her hip but she ignored the groceries while she made a careful inspection of the e-mail.

"It's kind of interesting that you let me see this," she said. "Most men would have hidden it. Even if it was totally innocent most men would have hidden it."

Duane looked at her calmly.

"No reason to hide it," he said, though, in a way, that was a lie. Hiding it had been his first instinct—only after he had thought it over did it seem better to leave the fact that he might see Honor out in the open.

Annie began to unpack the sack of groceries. She looked thoughtful. Duane watched CNN.

"Did you want to fuck her—your shrink I mean?" she asked. "That's what your daughters think you had in mind."

"My daughters are like their mother, and their mother was either black or white, sexual or not sexual. Karla didn't believe in gray areas."

"Then she wouldn't have known what to make of me—I'm kind of a walking gray area," Annie said. "You didn't answer my question. Did you want to fuck your shrink?"

"I fell in love with her," Duane admitted. "But she let me know right off that it was hopeless. I saw her with Angie Cohen a couple of times. They seemed like a happy couple."

"It might be interesting to meet Liz Landon," Annie said. "I assume that's Dr. Carmichael's new girlfriend. She really is a good painter. My granny owns several of her paintings, and my aunt Linda owns one or two."

She took the flank steak out of the refrigerator, where it had been marinating, and sniffed it.

"Hungry?" she asked. "I wish we had some fresh asparagus, but we don't."

Duane knew that the issue of his desire for Honor Carmichael was still hovering. He wanted to dispel it, and yet he knew he had to be cautious. Annie probably knew about his day of sex with Honor, though it was just possible that she didn't. But Annie was an analyst too, good, as she herself had put it, at finding out what was under the rocks. He wanted to say as little as possible about Honor to Annie. If he talked about it too much he'd end up giving himself away. The best plan was not to let Annie put him on the defensive.

It was a large flank steak, but the two of them finished it off rather quickly. Annie had brought home some German potato salad, some cheesecake, and a fresh bottle of bourbon. Soon enough the meal was over. They lay side by side on the couch, drinking the bourbon straight.

"I'm trying to be mature about Dr. Carmichael," Annie said. "Considering how deep your family's prejudice is against psychiatry, you must have been really sick—and knew you were really sick—to go to her in the first place."

"Yep," he said. "Karla fought it. In her opinion I had disgraced the family."

"Karla must have been a force of nature, but I can't tell that she was all that smart," Annie said. "Honor Carmichael's smart and I'm smart. I guess the best way to look at it is that Dr. Carmichael, whether you wanted to fuck her or not, sort of paved the way for us."

Duane liked it that she said "us." He wanted her to think of the two of them as joined.

"She knows my heart doctor," he said. "Maybe she can help me figure out what the tests mean."

"I don't think that's what this is about," Annie said. "If you wanted to fuck her so badly then that's mostly what this is about."

When bedtime came Annie ignored the futon and lay close beside Duane on the couch. Before coming to bed she put her sweats on over her pajamas, and her bathrobe on over the sweats.

"That's three layers of clothes you've got on," Duane pointed out. "Won't you burn up?"

"My problem," she said.

Sometime in the early morning, as he had expected, Annie woke up soaked in sweat. She sat up and flung off her bathrobe, sweats, and pajama top. Then she curled against him again.

In first light he listened to her steady breathing and watched the rise and fall of her young breasts.

31

"SPIT . . . good old spit," Honor said. "It's very underrated as a sexual aid."

She leaned over Duane and dribbled a mouthful of saliva over the head of his penis. Then she wet two fingers in her mouth and knelt over Duane, easing him into her. Once again they were woman-superior, only this time the act was occurring in a fine hotel in Boston. Honor rocked very gently, now and then tickling his scrotum.

After he came Duane ventured to ask about something he had noticed the minute Honor undressed. In the cabin she had had a superabundance of pubic hair—a heavy bush. Now she didn't. The bush had been reduced to just a sparse line of hair above Honor's cunt.

"What happened?" he asked, curious.

Honor saw where he was looking and flushed.

"Well, it's a little bit of a wicked story," she said. "We were in Paris and Liz wanted to spoil me, so she bought me the most expensive call girl in France—or maybe the world.

"Mademoiselle Nina," Honor went on. "She shaved me as part of the deal. I suppose if you spend a lot of time with your face in women's crotches muffs soon lose their appeal."

"I thought Liz was in love with you," Duane said. He didn't

want to come on like a country bumpkin, but he *was* a little shocked.

"Yes, and I'm in love with her, which is why this is probably the last time you and I can be together," Honor said. She knelt over him, nipples touching his chest—but she was watching his eyes.

"Liz is crippled," she added. "She's not able to be too ardent. So she bought me Nina."

Duane had only been able to manage a half erection, and yet Honor was able to hold him inside her—just. He felt that Honor was probably having sex with him to encourage him to address his heart problem—in other words, stay alive.

"I'm fifty-two," Honor said. "I can't attract beauties like Nina on my own. It's nice to have a lover who doesn't mind buying me pleasure, particularly if you're in Paris. It's hard not to want sex, if you're in Paris."

Duane slipped out, but Honor put him right back in—she seemed to enjoy just holding him inside her.

"You need to have that bypass operation pretty soon," she said. "In fact you should just go on and have it while you're here in Boston. If you'll do that I'll stick around a day or two to see that you're okay. Tommy Higginson thinks it's a case of the sooner the better."

Duane liked Dr. Higginson, who had put him through several tests, all of which pointed to the conclusion that Dr. Peppard and Dr. Calvert had come to in Wichita Falls. He did have ninety percent blockage in three important arteries, and he needed to have bypass surgery as soon as he could work it into his schedule.

Duane didn't admit that he really didn't *have* a schedule. He could have the operation anytime, but somehow he didn't feel like admitting that to Dr. Higginson—Duane told him he would look at his calendar and work out a date soon.

"I'll get around to it pretty soon," he told Honor, who now lay beside him, playing with his penis—occasionally she bent and took it in her mouth.

"I suppose I just have an adulterous heart," she told him. "I like lazy sex—the lazier the better. I love Liz Landon, but I also like sucking your cock. Will you lick me a little, if I make it easy for you?"

To make it easy, Honor squatted just above him. He licked, while Honor arched her back and grimaced pleasurably. He came. In the process he came half erect again. Honor knelt over him and put him back inside her.

They kept up their play until the sky outside their window darkened.

Then Honor sighed, got off him, showered, and dressed.

"There's a good clam house only three blocks from here. Ask the doorman," she said.

"You can't eat with me?"

"Not tonight—fortunately I ate my share of you this afternoon," she said. "You're not going to be stubborn about having the operation, are you?"

"Why would I be? I'll probably die pretty soon if I don't have it."

Honor considered him for a moment, her hand on the doorknob.

"Well," she said. "Though I'm not your doctor anymore there's something in your attitude that I don't really like."

Duane waited.

"You may be ready to die—I think that's what bothers me," she said. "Or you may *think* you're ready to die and procrastinate until you wait too long and have the big one."

"I won't do that," Duane said.

Honor looked at him a long time. Then she left, without speaking, without kissing.

He found that it no longer bothered him that they had not once kissed.

32

D UANE HAD ARRANGED with Bobby Lee to meet him at the DFW airport and drive him home. All the commuter flights to Wichita Falls were full that day, which was fine by Duane, who hated puddle-jumping airplanes.

For his part Bobby Lee hated anything resembling urban traffic—his whole life had been spent in a county with only one stoplight, and that merely a blinker. The rigors of the Dallas freeways horrified him—but he agreed to try to find Duane's terminal and gate. Bobby Lee's weakness was North Fort Worth barbecue, and Duane had promised him a free lunch at the pit of his choice if he would make the trip.

Duane had been looking forward to a little North Fort Worth barbecue himself. He stepped off the plane hungry, only to find Anne Cameron, sunglasses on her head, waiting at the exit gate for him.

"Your color is terrible," she told him immediately. "It's been terrible ever since I've known you, but I suppose I felt it wasn't my place to say anything about it. Now that we're living together I think I had better make it my place, or we won't be living together much longer because you'll be dead."

"I'm going to get the surgery—I just haven't figured out

when," he assured her. He bent forward to kiss her on the cheek but she raised her head and gave him a kiss on the lips that was so quick and hard that it was like a whiplash. Then she laced her fingers into his and led him across the street into the parking garage.

"What became of Bobby Lee?" he asked. "He usually won't pass up a chance to eat North Fort Worth barbecue."

For some reason Annie seemed angry—the set of her jaw was hard.

"He'll have to pass it up for the next few months because his wife shot him last night," Annie said. "She shot him in the stomach. He's not going to die, but it will be a while before he eats much barbecue."

"Good Lord," Duane said. "What was the fight about?"

"Porn."

"Porn?"

"Jessica caught him watching porn on her computer. At least that's the story I heard."

"Good Lord," Duane repeated. "I never knew Bobby to have much interest in porn."

Annie shrugged—she seemed slightly less angry.

"Earlene says Jessica's too freaked out by the prosthetic ball. She won't give him any sex."

"She knew about the fake ball when she married him," Duane said. "Why would she shoot him over a little porn?"

"She was *in* the porn and didn't want him to know it," Annie said. "I guess she's been making porn movies in a motel on the Jacksboro Highway for several months. Bobby Lee just happened to see one and recognized her. She claims he threatened her with a big wrench, so she shot him.

"Nice place, Texas," she added. "Even making the money I'm making I doubt if I could stay here another few months if I didn't have you to live with."

Duane was still hungry, but he didn't mention it—thanks to

his bad color he was pretty sure Annie wouldn't want him eating at any of the places he might have liked to eat.

The good news was that he actually *was* living with Annie Cameron. The bad news was that Bobby Lee was shot. For both of them North Fort Worth barbecue would have to wait.

On the drive home he dozed a little. Annie was driving very fast—he was just as happy not to know *how* fast. Annie's apartment was only up one flight of stairs, but the climb tired him. He regretted, a little, not having gone on and had the operation. If climbing one low flight of stairs tired him, then he was sicker than he supposed himself to be, and would have to plan accordingly.

There was a big box with a FedEx label sitting outside Annie's door.

"That's our salmon," she said. "I've just had it with horrible Texas food. From now on I'm going to fly in healthy stuff for us to eat. Fish, particularly."

Inside he saw that the counter by the cabinet was littered with glossy catalogues from food companies offering overnight delivery on a great many kinds of food.

Annie unpacked the salmon, put it in the refrigerator, grabbed her laptop, and was ready to go to work.

"Gotta go," she said. "I hate missing work, but I had to get you home."

"Thanks," he said. "I'll rest a bit and go see Bobby Lee."

"Don't overdo it," she warned. "I'll have a nice surprise for you, one of these nights—the nice surprise will be sex. I had my hymen perforated while you were gone."

Duane thought he must have misunderstood. Annie was twenty-six. Was she saying she was still a virgin?

"All three of my sisters had the same problem—tough hymens," she said. "We used to talk about doing a sitcom called *The Impenetrables*, about four sisters who couldn't quite get laid because their hymens were more than their boyfriends could deal with. I finally got tired of being poked at and adopted a medical solution, which I could have done long ago—only if I had, I'd have probably got pregnant by some asshole I didn't really want."

She was watching Duane closely, to see how he took this news. Mainly he just felt tired, very tired. The fact that Annie had fixed her hymen to make access easier for him didn't alarm him, but he was a little jet-lagged and the intimate news didn't arouse him, either. Mainly he wanted to lie down and he did, stretching out on Annie's ample couch.

She had been about to go out the door, but she turned and came back.

"Don't you die on me, Duane," she ordered.

"I won't," he promised.

She bent and kissed him lightly on the lips.

"You need to be gentle with me," she said. "I'm really just a kid."

Then she left.

33

BOBBY LEE LOOKED SAD, weak, frail. Always a small man, now he looked no larger than a child. They had not shaved him—his whiskers were white and stubbly. He was hooked to two IVs and complained bitterly about his catheter.

"Having a goddamned catheter jammed up your dick is the worst!" he said. "And all because I was fool enough to pick up a slut from Odessa and then marry her."

"I'm looking at some catheter time myself," Duane said. "Right now I'm just a heart attack waiting to happen. Both of us ought to be ashamed of ourselves."

"Ashamed of ourselves? Why?"

"What have either one of us done but make bad choices?" Duane asked. "In your case it's mostly been bad choices about women. In my case it's been bad choices about food."

"The way I see it the worst choice either of us made was to stay in Thalia," Bobby Lee said. "It don't take many smarts to figure out that Thalia's no place to spend your whole fuckin' life."

"True, but where would we have moved, if we *had* moved?"

Bobby Lee considered the question for a moment.

"Some place where the fishing was better," he concluded. "Maybe Possum Kingdom—or maybe Runaway Bay."

"Too close and not different enough," Duane said. "Why not the Florida Keys? Or Venezuela?"

"Venezuela's gone commie, from what I hear."

"Well, there's South Padre, if you're determined not to leave the country," Duane said. "There's places you can fish for flounder, and flounder is mighty good eating."

"Too close to the death squads," Bobby Lee reasoned.

"There's no death squads anywhere near South Padre," Duane insisted. "Karla and I used to go there. If there'd been a death squad she'd have death-squaded it right back."

"I once dreamed of living in Colorado," Bobby said. "Snow-capped mountains and pretty girls who could teach me to ski."

"That's more like it—Steamboat Springs is nice."

But Bobby Lee's mood took a sudden turn for the worse.

"Seeing Jesse in that porn movie just made me want her even more than I was already wanting her," Bobby Lee said. "That's crazy, isn't it? To want a slut like that?"

"I don't know about crazy," Duane told him. "You've always had a weakness for long-legged girls with big tits. But I do think you need to consider cutting Jesse loose. Next time she might aim higher."

Bobby Lee considered.

"Girls have threatened me with guns before but they never quite had the guts to pull the trigger," he said. "Old Jessica, she pulled the trigger. It's her Odessa background, I expect."

"Yes, and I'm glad you didn't die," Duane said. "I'll be by tomorrow."

"What about you, Mr. Walking Heart Attack? Can we expect wedding bells anytime soon?"

"No, I'm expecting bypass surgery," Duane said.

When he got home Annie was grilling the fish.

34

"IF WE EVER actually do the deed please remember not to stick your tongue in my mouth," Annie said.

It was late in the night—at first Duane wasn't sure whether he had heard her remark, or dreamed her remark. As usual Annie had gone to bed in three layers of clothes and then became too hot, so she sat up and shed the clothes. Soon she was topless again but not bottomless. She gave him a little kiss, no tongue involved.

"My father liked to French-kiss me and my sisters," she said. "I've hated tongues ever since and every stupid boyfriend I've had has immediately tried to stick a big slobbery tongue in my mouth. It's like having an eel in your mouth, when all you were hoping for was a nice little kiss—like this."

She gave him a nice little kiss, very soft, very tentative.

"So what did you do about your father? Did your mother know?"

"She didn't know and she wouldn't have been interested in knowing," Annie said. "I suppose she felt she owed Daddy children, so she must have let him do it once in a while—but I doubt she would have allowed him to stick his tongue in her mouth. Mom's fastidious—real fastidious. So am I. We're not easy women."

"If you were to go see your father tomorrow would he try to stick his tongue in your mouth?"

"You bet he would—but he won't get the chance. None of us will go near him unless there's a crowd around—like at a wedding or something."

Duane felt drowsy—he would just as soon have gone back to sleep and thought about Annie and her tongue-kissing father another time. But she was looking at him intently. Her eyes seemed to grow larger at night—she looked both seductive and childlike. He had never put his tongue in either of his daughters' mouths, but it seemed to him that if he had been drunk enough that kind of overstepping might have happened.

"Was that where it stopped?"

"Yep—no incest—I don't have *that* much excuse to be fucked up," she said. "My shrink says a zillion fathers do that. You'd think I'd get over it—but I still don't want you to put your tongue in my mouth if we should happen to be doing the wild thing some night."

"I won't," Duane promised. He yawned—he couldn't keep awake. He saw Annie raise her legs and slip off her panties and wondered if he was going to be expected to perform. He hoped not—he felt too weary, but a girl who had had her hymen perforated just for him might not want to wait.

But Annie merely snuggled close beside him. Then she sat up and fiddled with her Walkman—she needed to be taking in music day and night. It was not something he understood but it didn't bother him. His own children had the same need, though for mostly very different music. When he saw that Annie was more interested in the music than in him he relaxed and was soon dreaming of the ocean.

35

"I GOT NAKED last night—is that okay?" Annie asked.

Far from being naked at the moment, she was dressed for work.

"I think I remember that," he said. "Where are you going so early?"

"To Abilene, with Dickie—there's a little oil company for sale and we're going to look into it.

"There I was naked—it was your big chance to feel me up," she said, looking at him solemnly.

"The flight wore me out, I guess—I hope you're not mad at me."

"No, I didn't want you to feel me up," she said. "But there I was with my pussy exposed. It makes me wonder whether you're really attracted to me."

"I am," Duane assured her. "But sometimes at my age even when you're wildly attracted to someone who's willing to be naked with you, sleep just gets there first."

"Maybe you knew I didn't really want you to feel me up," she told him. "I get ambivalent. One minute I think I really want sex to happen and the next minute I don't.

"Maybe I don't really want the sex to happen but I'm hoping

you can manage to change my mind—does that make sense?"

"Annie, I'm going to try to change your mind," Duane said. "I think I might be able to—I just don't know when."

"That's nice," she said. "Maybe we can both have a nice surprise to look forward to.

"There'll be some fish arriving—halibut. I'll be home in time to cook it."

36

DUANE STAYED on the couch and tried to sleep but couldn't. He turned on the news but found he couldn't absorb it. He got up, shaved, and scrambled some eggs, which he ate with a peppery sausage he had bought from a Hispanic butcher on the north side of town. He ate the sausage but mainly just pushed the eggs around. He put a little bourbon in his coffee and was sipping it when Honor Carmichael called.

"I've been thinking of you too much and not in a good way," she said. "Last night I dreamed I read your obituary. Have you had sex with the little Cameron girl yet?"

"I had a fine opportunity just last night but I fell asleep," he said.

"You need to have the operation, Duane," she said. "It might do wonders for your sex life."

"I don't know that I care that much, anymore," he said.

"I don't think you *ever* cared that much—I'm speaking as your ex-shrink now," Honor said. "You're reluctant to come too close, even on the physical plane. I had my way with you and had it several times but you never managed a full erection the whole time."

"I was hoping you wouldn't notice, or wouldn't care."

"I *didn't* care and in fact I made it work pretty well," Honor said. "But then I'm fifty-two and I know what I'm doing. Probably Annie Cameron knows no more about sex than you do."

"I don't think she knows anything about it—maybe we'll be starting kind of even."

There was a silence on the line.

"When you came to me as a patient you were desperate—do you agree?"

"I was desperate—I just didn't realize it at first."

"That's because you were used to being the problem-solver, not the problem," she said.

"I know you saved me—nobody else could have," he said.

"No, I didn't save you—you aren't saved," she said. "Angie died just as you were beginning to let me in. Instead of saving you I fucked you, violating all my professional codes and rules. And now, even if I were still your doctor, I doubt you'd let me in."

He heard her blow into a Kleenex. She was silent for a bit.

"I wonder if you let Karla in—your wife of forty years."

Duane began to feel tired, very tired. He was so tired that he could barely hold the phone. The great fatigue he had felt when he first tried to reveal himself to Honor fell on him again, like a weight on his limbs, his brain, even his tongue.

"I'm real tired," he said.

Honor sighed.

"Okay, Duane . . . rest. I've no right to suddenly start trying to be your doctor again—I know that. And yet I feel like I had better make the attempt."

"You don't have to."

"Unless you have that operation you'll die pretty soon, and I don't think you mean to have it. You'll just stay there and play sweethearts with your Annie until she leaves for Asia. *If* she leaves for Asia."

Even in his deepening fatigue, Duane felt surprised at how smart Honor was. He had already decided for himself that he wasn't going to be operated on while Annie Cameron was still in Texas. He knew the operation might kill him, or at least leave him weak for a while, and he didn't want to lose the time with Annie. Honor had immediately figured that out—perhaps the detection of such strategies was child's play for a good psychiatrist. Anyway, there it was—he had to gamble on not dying in order to enjoy a few months with the young woman he was in love with.

"Annie hasn't really begun to want you—if she's capable of it," Honor said. "She's probably never been really aroused. Real sexual passion is probably ahead of her. If you're going to be the one to awaken her then you'll need to be able to get a real hard-on, one of these days."

To his surprise Duane realized that he was just then getting a real hard-on. His penis was swelling despite his fatigue. It was the thought of Annie in the throes of real arousal that caused the stiffening in his loins.

"I want you to think about your wife, Duane," Honor said. "I think you may have loved her and I've no doubt that you were good to her, in your way. But that's not the same as letting her in. I don't think you ever let her in."

37

DUANE BEGAN TO SLEEP for long stretches, day and night, no matter what was going on around him. Annie came whistling in after work and grilled the fish of the day—it was usually fish—and then she played on her computer while he rested and dozed.

"I don't really *have* to go off to Asia, honey," she said, one night. It was the first time she had called him "honey."

His spirits, low all day, lifted when she said it.

"I thought you wanted to go."

"I did—or I suppose I still kinda do—but I'm not the only geological analyst in the world. The Indonesians can easily replace me."

Duane felt that he was being offered something—and it was something he really wanted. But Honor Carmichael had put a troubling notion in his mind: the notion that he was, emotionally, a closed door. She even suggested that he had never opened that door even for Karla, his wife. The implication was that he had never let anyone in. What did it even mean, letting someone in? He wanted to think about it some more but first he helped Annie wash up their few dishes. Then she plopped down in his lap, kittenish, giving him little kisses, and commenting on the baseball game they were half watching.

"I love winners and hate losers," she said. "So naturally I love the Yankees, although most people hate them. And I love the Lakers—my family used to have seats just a few seats over from Jack Nicholson."

"Goodness me," Duane said.

"You want to get a bed? If we ever do the deed it might be good to have a bed to do it in. I'm getting too old for the futon life."

"Beds usually creak, when you're doing the deed on them," he pointed out.

"I suppose that's a point to consider."

They left the question of a bed unsettled and, when the ball game ended, turned off the light and slept on the couch. As usual Annie waited until Duane was sound asleep to get undressed. This time she left her panties on. She liked sliding in beside him, once he slept—it was like having a captive male to examine and explore.

Her nipples hardened and, just as they did, Duane opened his eyes. Annie felt as though she had been caught peeking. She got up and put a shirt on, but Duane had not really been awake, he had merely opened his eyes briefly and shifted his weight a little.

"What?" he asked.

Annie didn't say anything. She wanted Duane to stay asleep while she explored his body at her leisure. She felt naughty and a little shy. The first words she had spoken to Duane Moore had been about her nipples—yet now, even though they were living together, she felt too shy to want him to see her nipples stiffen. What was that about? She was beginning to feel aroused, and yet the last thing she wanted was for Duane to wake up and attempt to have sex with her. She was pretty sure she was going to want that someday, but she didn't want it yet.

When Duane was snoring steadily again Annie let her hand slide down his stomach—she left it there for a bit and then

146

slipped her hand under his underpants. She bypassed his penis and cupped his scrotum in her hand. There was a bulge in his underpants—his penis was thrusting against them. Annie watched. She couldn't quite see his dick but she liked holding his balls. She wanted to take his underpants off and watch his dick harden, but she didn't quite dare.

Duane, in slumber, sensed that his bedmate, Annie, was doing something pleasant, but it was a light awareness, not as deep as the slumber that held him in passivity.

As his stiffening penis began to strain harder against his underpants Annie touched his penis and tried to guide it through the slit he would use if he were trying to relieve himself. Somehow she could not manage this. His cock was bent in the wrong direction; she would need to take his underpants off, or pull them way down, and she didn't have the nerve. She had been told that once men were aroused beyond a certain point there was no stopping them: they had to have relief. Although she had begun to doubt the truth of this, she didn't want to test it with Duane—not just yet. She wanted him to teach her everything there was to know about sex, but she didn't want him to teach her just then, or maybe not even anytime soon. The design of his underpants irritated her—it ought to be possible to ease his dick through the slit but it wasn't working.

Annie gave up, and so did Duane's penis. It was half erect—she held it gently, hoping there was no harm in that. She lay very still. She didn't jiggle his cock—she just held it. She wondered if Duane would ever want her to give him a BJ, the act several of her boyfriends had been more or less obsessed with. She didn't oblige them though sometimes she wondered what cum tasted like. She also wondered if she would ever be close though to Duane to want him to put his mouth on her—the thought excited her, but her very excitement seemed to make her even more shy. She kept three fingers cupped around Duane's penis, which had become soft again. She let her cheek rest on his belly, and soon went to sleep.

In sleep Duane dreamed of a woman with hair under her arms. He dreamed he was poking himself into a slippery cunt—but before he could get fully in, the dream faded.

38

"UH-OH, did *I* make that happen?" Annie asked, in her sleepy-child voice. Semen had oozed over her fingers. Duane turned on the light. His penis was not erect, but it was oozing semen.

"I didn't know it was so gooey," Annie said. "Did I make it happen or what? I was just kind of holding you."

"I had a wet dream—maybe you helped bring it on. I was sound asleep. I don't know."

"Yuk, it's all over the couch—it's even in my hair! I thought when men came it was just a little squirt, but, man! You came like a gusher."

"It's what happens when you don't get regular sex," he said.

"Uh-oh, now I feel responsible," Annie said. She was blushing. "I haven't been giving you regular sex, or any sex, so you had to have an old messy wet dream."

"I'm not your responsibility, Annie," he told her. "And a wet dream is nothing to feel sorry about—wet dreams are real pleasant."

"I wish *I* could have one then—to reassure me," she said. "I never expected to wake up with cum in my hair. You're still oozing too."

"We could take a shower together," Duane suggested. "That

way we'd be clean and could finish off the night on the futon. To-morrow we can get the couch cleaned up."

In the shower Annie soaped Duane's dick two or three times, but still, now and then, a dribble of semen oozed out.

"How could you hold that much semen?" she asked. "I know I sound like a dope. Here I come on like a sophisticated California girl and I don't even know where semen comes from.

"I hope I'm not going to be too fastidious, like my mother," she added. "I never paid much attention to *The Joy of Sex* or man-uals or stuff, and of course my parents never said a word about sex to any of us. You must think I'm just a big fraud."

To his dismay, but not to his surprise, Annie began to cry. The shower was still on. The warm water sluiced over them as she cried. While he had his arms around her he got a half erection—Annie felt it poke against her.

"Hey—are you horny again already?" she asked.

"Not too," he said. "But here I am in a shower with a beautiful naked woman, and these things happen. Dicks are just apt to get hard when there's nakedness involved."

Annie did not seem particularly reassured, but they wrapped themselves in big towels and went to bed on the futon. Annie held him very close.

"Yeats has this poem, you know," she said. "'Crazy Jane Talks with the Bishop.' Ever read it?"

Duane shook his head.

"It's got a great last thought," Annie said: "'Nothing can be sole or whole that has not been rent.'

"I had my gyno do her thing with my hymen and all, but I'm still going to have to be rent, someday, you know. I hope it's you that does it."

"I hope so too," Duane said.

39

ABOUT MID-MORNING Dickie knocked. Annie had long since gone to work—Duane was watching an international soccer match on cable. He had never fully understood soccer but he liked to watch it anyway. The flow of movement up and down the green field relaxed him—he never got that much caught up in the score itself.

Duane had not been to his office in several days, although it was only five minutes away. He had no real part in the life of his oil company, anymore, and saw little reason even to check in.

"So are you living here now, Dad?" Dickie asked, surveying the dim apartment in which there was not a lot to see.

"Yep," Duane said. "I have a housemate who seems to like my company."

"Housemate?" Dickie asked, politely. Duane liked it that his son didn't challenge the term, as his daughters would have. For them cohabitation meant sex—that was that. But Dickie was more tolerant, and, also, more finely calibrated.

"Housemates so far," Duane said. "Not quite neutral but not quite lovers either. I love Annie but I feel like an old man."

"I think it's that you're a sick man," Dickie said. "You ate too many cheeseburgers, and now you need to let them fix your heart. Once that's done you may get randy again."

"Maybe, but even if that happens I may still feel too old for Annie."

"The girls think she'll marry you for your money, although I hear her family has a lot more money than we do."

"The girls are skeptical, like their mother."

"I wouldn't let their opinion bother you," Dickie said. "Where you're concerned there couldn't possibly be anyone good enough for you."

He was fiddling with his cigarette lighter, a sign that he was nervous.

"What do you really want to talk about?" Duane asked.

"Thalia," Dickie said. "Annie's finished over there, and Earlene retires next month. Jessica's run off from Bobby again, leaving him a broken man. He's put his house on the market."

"Uh-oh . . . where's he thinking of living when his house sells?"

"Lake Kemp—he's still got that shack, you know," Dickie said. "It's just a crappy house with a floor. I guess he means to retire and sit out there and watch teenage girls waterski."

"If Annie's through in Thalia what does that mean? Am I about to lose my housemate?"

"Doubt it—whatever's happening or not happening, you've taken her mind off Indonesia. I've given her a big office and of-fered her a big raise."

"To do what?"

"Reconnaissance," Dickie said. "She's always picking up tips from the petroleum industry Web sites. I got no patience with the computer stuff myself, but it's how money gets made in the oil business today."

"I ought to put our house up for sale," Duane said. "Would that bother anyone, you think?"

"Maybe Willy," Dickie said. "Willy's about the only grandkid with any attachment to Thalia. I was going to take our usual box at the rodeo next week, but it turned out that there are no Moores left who want to sit in a box at the rodeo."

"Not even you?"

"I'd go if I was here, but Annette and I are going to the Keys next week. I want to catch me a big fish."

"I think what you're saying is that it's time to close the Thalia office," Duane said. "I'm sure you're right. I'll drive over this afternoon and see if there's anything in it I might need."

"You might find a few pictures—otherwise it's already cleaned out."

"Do you like Annie?" Duane asked.

"I do like her—I hired her," Dickie reminded him. "And if you and her become more than housemates, I'd like that too. I don't really care what my sisters think."

"Thanks," Duane said. "Ever hear from your brother Jack?"

"I hear of him, not from him," Dickie said. "He's in Ecuador."

Dickie went out, closed the screen door and started to leave. But then he thought for a moment and came back inside.

"I meant it when I told you I liked Annie," Dickie said. "But even if I didn't like her—even if I thought she was a conniving cunt who was only after your money, I'd still be in favor of her staying with you, Dad."

"Why?"

"Because she might keep you alive," Dickie said. "Without her I think you'd die."

Then he left.

40

THE WEATHER was cooling. When he got ready to go to Thalia he considered, for a moment, riding his bicycle. He even rolled the bike around the courtyard of the apartment building a few times—then he put the bike away. He couldn't imagine himself riding a bicycle all the way to Thalia again, although he had ridden it in August heat the day he came back from Egypt. It had been a form of locomotion that had felt good for a while, but now it merely felt impossible. When he gave up on the notion he felt tired.

But when he drove south in his pickup he felt okay. Maybe when he got to Thalia he'd visit a bit with Lester Marlow, the retired banker with whom he had shared a lot of what might be called ups and downs. Maybe he would even pay his old cabin a visit, and stop off for a few minutes at the Asia Wonder Deli. He might even drive to Lake Kemp and see if Bobby Lee was already moved in to his insubstantial home.

All he took from his old office were two photographs—one of him holding up a large bass he had caught at a lake in East Texas; the other of himself and Bobby Lee, in oil-splattered overalls, standing by the best well they had ever brought in, 1,600 barrels a day. That had occurred in 1977. And after that, what?

When he left the old office and locked it he remembered how worried Karla had been the day they had rented it, forty years ago.

The rent was $150 a month—they worried that they might not be able to pay it—and there *had* been times when Duane could only cover the rent with poker winnings. Twice he had pawned his deer rifle and, at their lowest ebb, even pawned Karla's wedding ring.

Then things picked up. They brought in a few good wells—they learned how to operate economically. Three years after they rented the building, they bought it outright for $13,000. Ten years later they were prosperous enough to build the big house, which cost $60,000 and made them, unofficially, the richest family in Thalia, Texas.

The boom came and they learned to play tennis. They took trips to the gambling casino in Bossier City, Louisiana. The bust followed the boom but they weathered it, losing only one of their three rigs to the bank.

Children came, grandchildren came, and, rapidly, life passed. Karla head-oned with the milk truck. The kids and grandkids mostly moved to North Dallas. Dickie conquered his addiction and ran the company well. Jack roamed the earth. Duane walked a few years, then bicycled a couple. Now he was back in a pickup and the old Thalia office was closed.

When he walked out of the office he took only the two photographs and a yellow-handled pocketknife he had left in a drawer many years ago. It had just been a plain office—he had the feeling that he might be leaving it for the last time, yet all he could summon was a feeling of indifference. There should have been a big swell of emotion, like there was at the end of some movies; but in fact he had never particularly liked the office—it was drafty in the winter and the air conditioners rattled loudly all summer. He supposed he should have felt something like John Wayne felt as he left his post for the last time in *She Wore a Yellow Ribbon*—but he didn't. He stood on the porch for a minute, watching the thunderheads scuttle across the south plains.

Then he got in his pickup and left.

41

TWO BLOCKS from his office there was the big house. Duane started to drive past without stopping, but then he changed his mind and looked the house over for a few minutes. Already it seemed to him that it was becoming a sagging ruin. It needed reroofing, that was obvious. The woodwork needed painting. The plumbing was eroding.

Duane didn't want to go into the big house, but he was tired of having it on his mind. He got out and walked into the garage. He found an empty cardboard box, tore it up, and nailed part of it to one of the stakes that he used to tie up tomato plants. Then he wrote "For Sale By Owner" on the box with a Magic Marker. He wrote the drilling company's phone number on the box and drove the stake into the ground with a brick, hammering it into the soft dirt where tomatoes once had grown.

When he drove off he felt better. His hope was that the house would sell immediately.

Then he eased along two blocks west and stopped in Lester Marlow's driveway. Lester was sitting under a big shade tree, wearing only a bathing suit and a pair of flip-flops. It was the warm part of the day. Lester was shooting at several rows of dominoes that he had lined up on a nearby card table. The object of the game was to hit the lead domino and have it knock down the row. But Lester, despite careful aim, could not seem to hit the lead domino. Sometimes he didn't hit anything. Other times he hit the card table. Once in a while he hit a domino, which, somehow, fell in isolation.

"Hi," Duane said. "I just put my house up for sale."

"Why would you think I'd want your house, you louse," Lester said, jocularly.

"Just kidding," he added. "I just happen to remember that you built that house the year they put me in jail for embezzlement."

"You were only in jail one night," Duane reminded him. "And in county jail at that."

"You don't forget jail, though," Lester said. "I was worried all night that someone might try and cornhole me."

"Why, there was nobody else in jail at the time—I bailed you out, remember?" Duane reminded him.

"I know you've been a loyal friend," Lester said. "But I doubt that anyone will buy your house. Why would anyone who could afford a house like that want to live in Thalia as it is today?"

"He might if he was a drug dealer—be close to his work," Duane said.

Lester laughed mirthlessly and emptied his BB gun at the table with the dominoes. Not a single domino fell.

"How's Jenny?" Duane asked, referring to Lester's attractive, long-suffering wife.

"She's probably out at Lake Kemp, consoling Bobby Lee," Lester said. "Jessica's run off with another meth dealer."

"Why does Jenny need to drive all the way over to Lake Kemp to console Bobby?" Duane wondered.

"Well, she likes to console people and she can't console me because I have inconsolable angst," Lester said. "Bobby Lee just has common misery."

"You're not suggesting a romance between Jenny and Bobby, I hope?"

"I wish they would have a romance—be good for both of them," Lester said. "Hell, it would do me good too. Jenny and I've got nothing left."

They were silent for a moment, brought up short by contemplation of the muddle life had turned out to be.

"Did you close the office too?" Lester asked.

"Yep. Dickie's moved us to Wichita Falls."

"This whole town might as well move to Wichita Falls," Lester said. "There's really no reason for it to be a town anymore."

"Good point," Duane said.

When he drove away Lester was reloading his BB gun. Duane, not for the first time, wished he had not decided to visit his old friend, Lester Marlow.

42

DUANE FELT his spirits sinking—a direction they often took when he lingered in Thalia too long. He thought a milk shake might divert, or at least delay, a depression, so he pulled into the drive-thru at the Dairy Queen and, to his surprise, found himself being waited on by a cheerful young woman the color of a plum.

He had been a customer of the Dairy Queen since the day it opened, and had never been served by a nonwhite before. He smiled at the girl and she smiled back—that too was a novelty at the Dairy Queen, where the level of hospitality had never been especially high.

It might be, Duane thought, that fast food in the Thalia area was falling under Sri Lankan influence, which could only be a good thing.

He was just turning onto the dirt road that would have led him to the Asia Wonder Deli, when a familiar car, with a familiar woman in it, came racing toward him in a cloud of dust.

The woman was Jenny Marlow, and the car was surely one of the oldest surviving Volkswagens in the county, if not in the world.

Duane waved and Jenny braked. He pulled to the side of the road, got out, and strolled over to offer Jenny a kiss on the cheek.

She wore a cutoff T-shirt; her bony shoulders and freckled arms were bare. For some reason he had always been attracted to Jenny's bony shoulders.

"Running the back roads again, are you?" he asked. "I hope you're not peddling meth."

Jenny chuckled. "No," she said. "I just can't resist the crab rolls at the Asia Wonder Deli. Want one?"

"Actually I was headed for the Asia Wonder Deli myself," Duane said. "It's about the only reason to drive this dusty old road."

"Agreed," Jenny said. She had prominent front teeth—another thing about her that Duane had always found attractive.

"I hear you're nursing Bobby," he said. "That's a saintly thing to do."

"I'm not doing it in a saintly fashion, though," Jenny said, "Bobby Lee and I are one another's last resorts. We've been one another's last resort for longer than I care to remember."

Duane had no comment on that. There was more than one way to be someone's last resort, he knew. Just having a cheerful woman to say hello to you at the post office every morning for forty years would be a good kind of last resort. And if, occasionally, a little sex was involved, then so much the better.

"I hope you took the trouble to visit Lester," Jenny said. "We never see you now but you're just about our oldest friend in this slipping-down town. I'd be hurt and so would he if you showed up in Thalia and didn't come to see us."

"Jenny, I'll always come and see you—next time I'll bring Lester some BBs for his airgun."

"That's nice for Lester, but what will you bring me, honey?" she asked.

Jenny had always been bold in speech—the two of them had flirted for many years but he didn't remember that it had ever gone past flirting—though he wasn't entirely sure. During the heady days of the boom, in the 1970s, he was often drunk and had been led into brief amorous affairs with two or three women—encounters that now were a blur in his mind. Had he slept with Jenny Marlow once or twice? He knew Karla had disliked her, on no better grounds than her suspicion that Duane was attracted to Jenny's bony shoulders and big front teeth. Did they or didn't they? It was one of those questions he would probably never know the answer to.

"You could bring me a hard-on, someday," she said. "I wouldn't look askance at it, if you were to. I'm driving lots of these long country roads and not getting very damn much."

"That might be easier said than done," Duane allowed.

Jenny grinned her toothy grin. "I was mostly teasing," she said. "But I wasn't *entirely* teasing."

"I guess there's such a thing as waiting too long," Duane said. "Bobby Lee ain't gonna drown himself is he?"

"Good news on that front," Jenny said. "Jessica got busted in Broken Arrow, Oklahoma, with a station-wagonful of drugs. Bobby swears he won't bail her out this time, and if he won't nobody will. Maybe we've seen the last of Jessica for a while."

"I hope so—I guess I'll mosey along and get my crab puffs," Duane said.

"Don't forget my present, next time you're over," Jenny said, grinning at him.

Then she tooted her horn and drove off.

Duane wondered if she had meant what she said. More likely, he thought, she was just pulling his string.

43

DUANE TRIED not to look at the litter in the bar ditches as he drove out toward his cabin. Once, the trash in the bar ditches made him angry—he was highly incensed by the general slovenliness of the people who drove the road: cowboys, roughnecks, hunters, drug dealers had once angered him so that he spent hours each week doing his best to patrol the ditches and remove the trash. It had given him what Honor called focus, and he worked at it industriously for more than a year.

He had only been away a rather short time, but it seemed to him that the volume of debris was much higher than it had been when he left for Egypt. What that probably meant was that more meth dealers were using the road for their nocturnal cooking of this cheap and deadly drug.

The sight of the trash—bottles, cans, plastic sacks, a wash tub with a hole in it—annoyed him as it always did but he went on to the cabin without picking up any of the trash. The trash would have to wait until after his operation—he fully meant to clean it up, but not until after he had rid himself of the strange fatigue that made his limbs feel so heavy.

When he came to his cabin he felt so heavy that he didn't even go in. The cabin had been his refuge and his peace for more than two years. It was the one place where he felt calm, safe and functional, deeply at ease.

But now it just looked like a dusty, empty frame cabin, on a rocky hill.

The moral, if there was a moral, was that no one place was sufficient for all the stages of his life. His needs, like the needs of most people, changed and varied.

Duane didn't want to be on his hill anymore—didn't care about his cabin. He wanted to be with Annie Cameron. Duane turned his pickup and drove home fast, skipping the Asia Wonder Deli. Crab rolls could wait. He was hungry, but not for crab rolls or barbecued pork. He was hungry—really hungry—for his girl.

44

WHEN DUANE walked into the pool area of their apartment he found Annie by the pool, smoking and crying. He had never seen her smoke before—the sight was a shock, though he couldn't have said why, since the oil patch generally was like a national sanctuary for smokers. He himself had smoked much of his life and didn't regard it as much of a vice, certainly not in comparison to the drugs that were readily available in the oil patch generally.

Annie was alone in the pool area. She wore a red bikini—the cups sat on her small breasts, giving a sad effect. She didn't sunbathe much—her chest was freckled. The minute she saw Duane she jumped up and threw her arms around him. Her bikini top fell off but there was no one to see her but Duane.

"What's wrong?" he asked.

Annie was sobbing so hard that he couldn't tell whether she heard the question. She flipped her cigarette butt into the pool, which was a no-no but, for the moment, he was too concerned with getting her calmed down to worry about one cigarette in a swimming pool that nobody seemed to be using.

He led her carefully up the stairs and into their apartment—he had come to think of it as theirs, rather than hers.

"Hey, what's wrong?" he asked again.

"I thought you left me!" Annie sobbed. "You're always here when I come home, but I got off early today and came to get the fish started and you weren't here."

"But this is the time you usually get home and I *am* here," Duane pointed out. Annie's chest was still heaving.

"Don't try to be reasonable with me!" Annie said sharply. "This is not reasonable. I know it's the time I usually get home. But when I did get home and you weren't here the apartment looked so empty that I got scared."

"I was in Thalia. Dickie came by and said he was closing the old office, so I went over and had a look. I visited with Lester Marlow a few minutes. I meant to go to the Asia Wonder Deli but I got such a hankering to see you that I just came on home."

"Let's don't cook the salmon right now," she said. "Let's have sex."

She put her hand on him and squeezed, rather roughly.

"Ouch," he said, in a teasing tone—he knew by now that Annie was too inexperienced to know what she was doing sexually—she didn't yet understand how sensitive the male equipment was.

Annie didn't seem to hear him. She stripped off her bikini bottom, squeezed herself against his thigh, and kissed him—a light kiss, not the hungry kiss that might lead into immediate sex.

Rather than feeling aroused, Duane felt stalled—uncomfortable to a degree with Annie's sudden invitation.

"Whoa!" he said. "Let's talk a minute."

Annie sniffled and let go of his penis.

"I don't think you want me," she said. "I never did think you wanted me."

"I *do* want you—but you're upset," he said. "I want you to calm down—I'll help you make dinner and then we'll see about sex."

She looked at Duane hostilely.

"I said I wanted to have sex," she said. "I wish you would just take me at my word and fuck me, no discussion," she said. "Why do we have to talk?"

Duane knew that he didn't really have the words to placate her—anything he said would just make her more angry. He put his hand on her, as if to give in, and found that she was completely dry. Instead of opening to his hand she tightened against it.

"I don't know what to do," he admitted. "Could we just sit on the couch for a minute and maybe have a drink?"

"Are you so scared of me you have to get drunk to do the deed?"

"I don't know about the deed, Annie," he said. "I don't know about doing it right now. We sleep together every night. It's not hard to slip into doing the deed when you're in bed with a beautiful woman."

"I'm not beautiful—I'm just okay and I've got no boobs."

Duane went to the cabinet, got the whiskey and two glasses.

"I want my drink," he said. "This is the cocktail hour, which comes before the sex hour," he said—he was trying for a bit of humor. But Annie didn't smile—she was standing naked, right where she had dropped her bikini bottom. He got some ice cubes and poured the whiskey over them. When he handed Annie a glass she accepted it.

"The sex hour can be anytime two people want to fuck," she said. "I guess you don't, really."

"And all this is because I wasn't right here when you stepped in the door?"

Annie shrugged. She went and got a shirt and a pair of cutoffs. She sipped some of the whiskey and gradually the tight look went out of her face—she looked like a confused child, but at least she was calming down.

"My mother says that if you're not actually fucking a man he's always apt to leave you," she said. "Since we're not actually fucking I came in and saw you weren't here and chose to believe the worst."

"Along that line there's something you might want to consider," he said. "Your mother could be full of shit."

Annie smiled her real smile—a smile of girlish delight.

"Right on, partner," she said.

45

"CAN YOU EVER ORDER steaks from these overnight catalogues?" Duane asked, although he knew the answer. Left to himself during the day he often browsed through catalogues offering
big thick porterhouses and excellent K.C. sirloins.

"Of course you can order steaks," Annie said. "But why would
you if you have a ninety percent blockage in three major arteries."

She laid out a dill dip with the salmon. It was supposed to be
wild Atlantic salmon and proved tasty. Duane had his doubts
about the wildness but kept them to himself.

"Didn't you just get irrationally upset because I wasn't here the
minute you stepped in the door?" he asked.

Annie looked at him defiantly.

"What was so irrational?" she asked. "You *will* leave someday,
unless we get ourselves a sex life."

"You think having a sex life guarantees that people will stay
together?"

Annie didn't like the question, so she didn't answer it.

"What's your opinion?" she asked.

"I don't think anything guarantees that people will stay together," he said. "Lots of people who are having sex lives, and
pretty good sex lives, don't stay together."

"Oh fuck it! I don't want to talk about it anymore," she said. "I just want to feel like a woman rather than a girl. Maybe if we had sex I'd feel like a woman."

"How'd we get from steaks to sex?"

"If you're just going to start eating steaks then you must be suicidal—what am I even doing living with you?"

"It's just that I like a steak, once in a while," he said. "I doubt that a steak every week or so is going to push me into a heart attack."

"It could," Annie insisted.

So could sex, Duane thought, but he didn't say it. He was beginning to suspect that Annie Cameron had never really had sex—or never had full intercourse at least. Since he had moved in with her she had often talked about boyfriends who had tried to stick their tongues in her mouth or their dicks into her cunt but these complaints didn't entirely ring true. The stories seemed like a subterfuge, all aimed at keeping him from discovering the truth, which was that Annie was essentially virginal. Probably there had been efforts at penetration, but had any of them worked? He didn't know.

When they got up from the table Annie pointedly gathered up all the catalogues from overnight steak-suppliers, took them downstairs and threw them into the dumpster. It amused him but also annoyed him a little.

"What do you expect that to accomplish?" he asked. "There's a steakhouse six blocks from here. I can always get a steak if I want a steak."

Annie ignored the comment.

"Could we take a shower together?" she asked. "I like taking showers with you. It's like we're under a waterfall together," she said, stripping right where she stood but then carefully picking up her clothes and folding them.

In the shower she stood as close to him as possible and

reached down and grabbed his dick again. It came half up and she soaped it thoroughly.

"Is it a turn-off that I'm so compulsive about germs?" she asked.

"Nothing you do is a turn-off. Pretty much everything you do is a turn-on."

He reached back and increased the volume of cold water in the shower, which had the immediate effect of causing her nipples to pucker. He rubbed them a little while they were puckered, which startled Annie—she produced a little gasp.

"You never touched my nipples before."

He continued to caress them lightly. Then he made the water warm again and they held one another close for several minutes.

"I'm going to shave that stupid hair under my armpits," she said. "Why should I imitate Jeanne Moreau?"

Once they dried off Annie did shave the hair under her armpits.

"What if I shaved my pussy—would that excite you?"

"Annie, I *am* excited. You don't need to do a thing but come to bed."

When she did come to bed he reached between her legs and began a very slow caressing—he felt her nipples pucker again, and, again, she gave a little gasp. Duane kept on, slowly rubbing a finger up and down her slit, up and down. He touched the little sheath over her clitoris—just a touch, which provoked a louder gasp. He kept rubbing until, eventually, she began to lubricate—but only a little. He dribbled a little saliva on one finger and gently pushed it into her.

"Why'd you have to put spit in me?" she asked. "I don't like spit."

"Why not? It's clean and it's useful."

"Just stick your dick in—you don't have to use spit," she said. She took hold of his penis again and squeezed it—he felt swollen but he knew he was not really erect. So he continued to caress Annie's slit, which began to get a little wetter. She was still very tight. He had his finger in only to the first knuckle—when he tried to push farther in he had to push hard.

"Ouch," Annie said. "Can't you just take your finger out and put your dick in?"

He took his finger out and knelt above her for a moment—he had only the beginnings of an erection; when he he tried to penetrate Annie he got no farther than his finger had gotten. Then he became flaccid and slipped out.

"I'm sorry," he said. "I shouldn't have been in such a hurry."

"I guess you're just impotent—bummer," Annie said.

"That's not the whole story," he said, putting his hand on her again. He put a finger in and, as he did, felt his penis rise a little. Annie was wetter now. He put a second finger in and in—she gasped but didn't protest. She was gripping his fingers tightly—too tightly.

"If you'll let go for a minute we might get lucky," he said.

She let go and he eased himself into her—he didn't have a full erection but he made a partial entry and gave Annie a moment to adjust to him.

"I don't know about this—you're kind of big," she said.

Staying where he was he began to rub her labia.

"Oh gee, yeah," she said, and gave him a light kiss. "Oh gee . . ." Some tone or her little gasps aroused him and he was soon in almost full erection.

"Oh gee . . . maybe you better come out—it hurts," she said.

"What was that you were reading me from some poem?" he asked.

"You're right—I gotta tough this out," she said. "This is the part where I get rent . . . ooh!"

She seemed to tighten even more around him and in a moment he felt himself come. It took Annie a moment to realize what had happened. Duane was gushing into her, though only briefly.

"I guess you put a lot of goo in me," she said. "I don't like semen very much—it's going to drip on the couch."

"It's just protein," Duane said.

"Didn't you want me to come too?" she asked, looking hurt.

"Of course I did—and I do," he said. "But this takes practice—you're just starting out."

"You didn't fuck me very long," she said, reproachfully.

"No, I didn't," he said. "I'm sorry. But we're at different stages: you're just starting out and I'm just finishing up. We'll get better at it and one day soon you'll get there."

"You mean have an orgasm—I doubt it," Annie said. "My mother's never had one. My sister Spence claims to have had one but she's a fucking little liar. I don't think any of us has had one. There's just something wrong in the Cameron family."

"There's nothing wrong with you," Duane said. "You're just inexperienced. I have to learn what you really like."

She looked at him with a sly smile.

"You think you'll live long enough to find out what I really like?"

"I hope to."

"Then you better lay off the steaks, buddy, " she said. "That's all I've got to say."

46

THE NEXT DAY, in an effort to recover his energies, Duane got up when Annie did. They showered together—that was getting to be one of Annie's favorite things—but, apart from a little nuzzling, didn't indulge in any sex play. Annie was compulsive about not being late for work.

It surprised her that Duane got dressed, as if he were going to work too.

"I'm going to see Bobby Lee," he said. "I'll probably be back before you are, but if I'm not don't worry."

"I won't be worried but I might be pissed," Annie told him. "I might want to try a little more of that sex stuff."

"We can try it," Duane said. "It may be that the more we play around the more you'll come to like it."

Annie thought that over. She gazed at the couch, as if trying to remember exactly what they had done.

"It hurt a little but I guess I did like it," she said. "It felt real, at least. It was messy because you shot all that goo into me but at least I really wanted you. I think that was the first time I really wanted you."

"That's good to hear," he said, and they left.

Duane had not been to Bobby Lee's crappy house for years and had to poke around among the many inlets of the large lake before he found him. When he did find him it was because he spotted Bobby's new red pickup.

Bobby Lee, wearing an undershirt and cutoffs, was down at the water's edge, where he had just caught a small green turtle. He seemed uncertain as to what to do with the turtle.

"I'm getting tired of catching these little green bastards," he said to Duane, without preamble.

"Then you may have to give up fishing," Duane said. "Catching turtles is just part of the fishing experience."

Bobby cut the hook and pitched the turtle back into the lake.

"Did you bring your rod?" he asked.

"Forgot it."

"You can use Jessica's," Bobby Lee said. "She only used hers once and got her hook stuck in her ankle that time."

"I hear Jessica's going up for a while," Duane said.

"A while is right—she had a whole carful of dope," Bobby said. "I'm forced to face the fact that my beautiful wife is a goddamn drug dealer."

"Let's go out in the boat," Duane suggested. "I need to sit and look at water—it might soothe me a little."

Bobby Lee had a small boat with an old outboard that had to be carefully coaxed into life, but he eventually got it going and they were soon far out in the middle of a very large lake. The water was brown. Lots of turtle heads protruded from the murky surface.

"A game warden came by and told me they figure there's thirty thousand goddamn turtles in Lake Kemp alone. There's plenty in Kickapoo and Arrowhead too. Why do turtles flourish when I don't?"

Duane put a little stink-bait on a hook and cast a few times. Nothing took the stink-bait but a perch much too small to keep.

"How long will Jessica be in the pen?" Duane asked.

Bobby shrugged.

"Probably six or seven years," he said. "I should be over her before she comes out, but of course there's no guarantee."

"Let's hope you're over her—how about you and Jenny?"

Bobby Lee smiled.

"Jenny's my salvation," he said. "If we hadn't had a little itch for one another I'd have had to get through life with hardly any sex at all."

Duane was still trying to remember whether he had ever slept with Jenny Marlow—it would have had to be in the 1970s, during the boom, when he and Karla had both strayed. He thought he remembered being in bed with a woman with bony shoulders and big front teeth, but there were several women of his acquaintance who shared those attributes. His memories of Jenny might only have been a fantasy, and, anyway, it was not a matter he needed to discuss with Bobby Lee.

"How are you and Miss California?" Bobby asked.

"We're doing better—I'm pretty smitten," Duane said.

Bobby didn't pursue the matter.

"Why do you suppose life's got so muddled up?" he asked. "I've been confused at times through the years but I don't remember being this muddled up."

"In my humble opinion you've always been muddled up, Bobby," Duane said.

He caught another perch and decided he was tired of fishing.

"Hungry?" he asked.

"I'm hungry—where do you want to eat?"

"Pat's," Duane said.

Pat's was a steak house in the nearby town of Seymour. It was run by a woman named Pat who believed in smearing her steaks with lots of butter. Duane ate a T-bone and then ate another—an indulgence that caused both Pat and Bobby Lee to lift an eyebrow.

"Has somebody been starving you, honey?" Pat asked.

"No, but somebody's been feeding me a lot of fish," he allowed.

"His arteries are all blocked up," Bobby Lee explained. "He must be feeling suicidal or else why's he eating two steaks?"

"I doubt it will hurt him—my steaks are lean meat," Pat said.

"How lean's all that butter," Bobby asked.

"It's just that everything tastes better with a lot of butter on it," Pat explained.

On the way back to the crappy house Bobby Lee kept looking at Duane.

"You had to sneak off to eat those steaks, didn't you?" he asked finally.

"Spoken like an old sneaker-offer."

"If you have to sneak off to eat red meat I don't know what to think about your new relationship."

"Nobody asked you to do much thinking about my new relationship," Duane pointed out.

"I know, but I like to imagine that your life is better than my own," Bobby Lee said.

"Karla always said it was dumb to suppose that other people's lives are better than your own," Duane said. "Her opinion was that most people are about equally miserable."

"Is Annie Cameron miserable?"

"No—I don't think she's miserable," he said.

"Then that shoots Karla's theory all to shit—don't it?" Bobby Lee said.

Duane's eyelids had began begun to feel heavy.

"Hope you don't mind if I take a nap," he said.

"Let me ask you a question, before you nod off," Bobby Lee said. "It's pretty personal. I wouldn't want you telling anybody I asked."

"Just ask it—I need my nap pretty soon."

"Do you think Viagra would work for a man with only one ball?"

"Gosh," Duane said. "I don't know. How would I know?"

Then he immediately began to wonder if Viagra would really work for a man with two balls and a few clogged arteries. He had seen plenty of Viagra ads and yet had never applied them to his own situation, which was the situation of a largely impotent man in love with a woman much younger than himself.

"Gosh," he said again, wondering how he could have entirely missed the possibility that this well-known remedy for erectile dysfunction might be able to improve his own performance with Annie Cameron.

"Let's make a secret pact," he suggested. "I'll try it if you'll try it. Maybe one of us will get lucky."

"Maybe both of us will get lucky," Bobby Lee said. "I just feel I ought to be doing a little better with Jenny than I am in the here and now."

"I know the feeling," Duane said.

47

WHEN HE LEFT the lake Duane went straight to his doctor and asked about Viagra. His MD was a middle-aged woman named Hunnicut, who immediately handed him a bunch of free samples.

"It seems to work for some people," Dr. Hunnicut said, with a sigh. "Unfortunately it didn't work for Freddy, except once. It's a good thing I've got a healthy sense of humor."

Duane knew that Freddy was Dr. Hunnicut's husband—they had met once or twice at barbecues. Freddy had never seemed happy—he was a moper.

"Aren't you going to ask me about the once?" the doctor said, with a wry smile.

"I'll bite, I guess," Duane said.

"If you've seen the commercials you might have noticed the small print about what to do if you have an erection that lasts four hours or more."

"Uh-oh."

"That's right. Freddy usually couldn't get it up with a fork lift, but he took his Viagra for a while and came up with one of those four-hour erections.

She cackled at the memory—then she sighed.

"I sometimes think the sexual organs were put there to keep

the human race humble," she said. "They've certainly kept me humble."

"What'd Freddy do about the long hard-on?"

"Went to the ER and got a muscle relaxant—Freddy's easily embarrassed. I don't think he'll ever get over that experience."

"I hope it don't happen to me," Duane said. "That would be too much of a good thing."

"Just go to the ER, if it happens. They see two or three cases a night, even here in stodgy Wichita Falls.

"It's amazing how reluctant people are to give up on sex," she added. "It feels good and, if you're married, it appears to be free."

"It's not really free, though, is it?"

"Not really," the doctor said.

48

DUANE LEFT his Viagra samples on the kitchen counter. He wanted Annie to see them the minute she walked in. He didn't want her to think he was complacent about their halting, partial sex life.

She did notice them the minute she walked in.

"Well, my, my," she said, giving him a light kiss. "Viagra the wonder drug. Savior of old farts who can't get it up."

"Like me," Duane said.

"I wonder—I wonder."

"You wonder what?"

"It may be a blessing that you have a little bit of erectile dysfunction, if that's the phrase."

"Doesn't feel like a blessing to me," he said.

"Yeah, but keep in mind that I'm really just a beginner," she reminded him. "I'm a beginner who needs to go slow. I may need the slightly impaired approach."

Duane listened.

"If you'd been all rampant and just poked your big dick into me like most men would have I might have hated the experience, and thrown you out."

Duane just listened.

"It's complicated, right?" she said, kissing him again. "But I'm on your side—or maybe it's *our* side—and I have a little surprise for you too."

"What?"

She reached into her bag and pulled out a video in a white case.

"It's a how-to video. I've already checked out the couple and they're beautiful. They're nothing like the actors in those grunty porn movies."

There was a picture of the instructors on the cover of the video. They were in a close embrace.

"Let's take a shower and let's eat some linguini and let's watch this video," Annie said. "I may want us to try some of the things they do if that's okay."

"I can't wait," Duane said.

49

THE MINUTE THEY SLIPPED *The Techniques of Intimacy* into the VCR and an attractive, naked couple faced them, smiling, Duane knew that Annie's response to sex was about to change.

"Where'd they find those two?" she wondered. "Are there people who apply for jobs as sex instructors, or what?"

"I wonder about that myself," Duane said.

"I think his dick's shorter than yours," she said. Even though the young couple on the screen were just standing there Annie's breath had become a little raspy. They sat on the couch, Duane in an undershirt and briefs, Annie in a robe.

"Those two could be our next-door neighbors," Annie said, "if our next-door neighbors just happened to be really nice-looking sex instructors."

A female voice introduced the couple as Jane and Jim and said a few words about sexual fulfillment being the key to a happy marriage. The voice spoke of the pleasure bond, and stressed that ignorance of the techniques of intimacy could damage what might otherwise be a happy relationship.

Then Jane took Jim's penis in her hand and cupped his scrotum—an erection soon appeared, allowing Jane to demonstrate the proper way to put a condom on your partner. The dangers of unprotected sex were stressed, and AIDS came in for a brief mention.

Then Jane and Jim were in bed, kissing. The voice intimated that intimacy should be enjoyed slowly—couples who hurried often failed to achieve a full response.

"She means coming," Annie said. She gripped Duane's cock, a little too tightly.

Following the kissing Jane and Jim paused to give the viewer a brief anatomy lesson: here, in Jane's case, were the labia, here the entrance to the vagina, here, above, just a little white speck, the clitoris—and, as for Jim, here were the glans penis, the testicles, the scrotum.

"I wish they'd do it," Annie complained. "I don't need this whitebread anatomy stuff. I know where my cunt is."

Then, before Annie could complain anymore, Jane and Jim began to have intercourse, slow at first but then more vigorously.

"Look how hard her nipples are—this is the real thing," Annie said. "Oops, he came out."

Jim had come out, but was quickly reinserted by Jane. Annie began to breathe more heavily. Jane and Jim had been using the missionary position, but then, suddenly, Jane put her legs against Jim's shoulders.

"Oh shit, that's hot, I wanta do that," Annie said. "You want to turn the TV off and do it?"

"Let's watch a little more, they might do something even wilder," Duane said. Jane's white legs were widely splayed beside Jim's straining body. Annie's breath was hoarse. Duane put a hand on her and discovered that she was wet—far better lubricated than she had been the day he tried to enter her.

But meanwhile, on the screen, Jane had turned over, her butt elevated, her face in a pillow. The calm voice mentioned that some couples liked an anterior approach, an approach sometimes known as doggy style. There hung Jane's swollen pudenda—she reached around under herself, to guide Jim in.

"I want to do that—I want to do that right now," Annie said. "It seems so degrading but it's hot, isn't it?"

Duane didn't answer. On the screen Jim's balls were slapping against the back of Jane's thighs. Duane slipped two fingers into Annie. The passage was tight, but not as tight as it had been the night before.

Then Jane and Jim demonstrated a woman-superior position, which did little for Annie.

"I don't like seeing her boobs bounce like that," she said.

The woman-superior was followed by a side-by-side position which allowed Jane to stroke Jim' s penis as it went in and out of her. Jim, for his part, was rubbing the sheath that hid Jane's clitoris.

"The clitoris ought to be bigger—no wonder guys sort of miss it," Annie said.

Duane realized that he had a full erection. Annie was on her back, her bathrobe fully open. Duane urged her to lift her legs and rest them against his shoulders. When he began to push into her, Annie gritted her teeth for a moment. "Just be real slow," she said.

Duane obeyed, though he knew that if he went too slow he might lose his erection. He pushed on in, slowly, as Annie squeezed her eyes shut and panted heavily.

"It's too tight," she said. "You must have the biggest fucking dick in the world."

Finally he was completely seated in her, something he had feared might never happen. He moved a little, not much—just a little in and out—when, to his surprise—he had not expected it to happen for weeks, if ever—Annie came, in a series of hard jerks in which she pounded her pelvic bone against him. She cried out three times. Then she gasped and gasped, as she drew in long breaths. On the screen Jane had Jim's prick in her hand and was about to demonstrate the technique called fellatio. Duane found the remote and switched off *The Techniques of Intimacy*—it had

served its purpose. Annie, still gasping, her chest heaving, had gone limp.

Duane felt a sudden tiredness. He stayed in Annie as long as possible, although one of his legs began to throb.

"More goo," Annie said, giving him a light kiss, as he slipped out.

"You got me to come—I love you," she added.

"The video helped," Duane pointed out.

"I still think I might go for that anterior stuff—I may want you to fuck me doggy-style," she added.

Duane felt a terrible tiredness, and the pain in his leg grew sharper. His heart was racing.

"Doggy-style's gonna have to wait," he said.

"Why, honey? Why can't we do it now?"

"I may have overdone it," Duane admitted. "I don't feel right. I think I may need an ambulance."

"Oh my God—okay, okay. One fuck and look at you," Annie said.

50

THREE MONTHS after he underwent triple bypass surgery at Wichita Falls Regional Hospital, he and Annie Spence Cameron were married, in a house belonging to her parents, in Patagonia, Arizona.

Annie's three sisters were present, but not her parents—they were yachting in the Greek islands and chose not to interrupt their trip.

Except for Jack, reportedly in Ecuador, all Duane's children and grandchildren came, though his daughters, by this time, had decided that they hated Annie.

That winter Annie's parents gave her the Patagonia house as a wedding present. Annie had taken Duane there as soon as he was able to travel. They walked every day in the desert. At night they sat by wood fires. The area abounded in quail and dove. Annie was an excellent wing shot. Sometimes they had quail for dinner, sometimes dove. Annie was not squeamish about dressing small game.

Their house was on a hill, in sight of Mexico. Duane spent most of his days on the long deck, covered in an old blanket if it was nippy. Even when it was nippy it was sunny. He liked to sit on the deck, looking toward Mexico. Annie was in and out, checking on him. She and Dickie had formed a futures trading company, which involved a great deal of computer time for Annie. Evidently they were successful. One day Annie told him she was worth three million dollars, which was about the most Duane had ever been worth, and then only in the boom.

In Duane's eyes Annie seemed to grow more beautiful month by month. In his eyes she was perfect. Where he was concerned, her attention never faltered.

Yet, within the good order of their marriage, there was a sadness. In Duane's view he had only survived the operation in a technical sense—someone lived and breathed within his body but was it he? He never again felt that he was quite who he had been, but he didn't try to explain this to Annie, his lovely, sparkling wife.

Annie's sadness—well, he didn't really know what Annie's sadness was about. They sometimes tried to joke about their sex. Annie's first orgasm had very nearly been his last orgasm—indeed, his last anything. Both of them were aware that he was a wounded man—his doctors told him to be careful for a while, not to overdo. But it was hard not to overdo when you had a wife as young and responsive as Annie. Sometimes, cuddled by the fire, Duane would arouse her with his fingers—she would have a little climax and bite his shoulder. Once casually naked, now she was modest, likely now and then to expose a breast but not her cunt. When Duane tried to persuade her to let him put his mouth on her she shrugged him off.

"It's just that you're way down there—too far away. I'd rather hold you," she said. "And you know how I am about tongues, anyway."

He had, for some reason, let his Viagra samples lie. But after a time Annie prodded him into trying it.

"All couples have some problems," she said, maturely. "Just take your pills. In a year or two you might be as good as new."

In the spring after his operation Annie had to go to Davos, Switzerland, to a high-level conference involving the petroleum industry. In the weeks before her trip she worried and fussed constantly about leaving him.

To reassure her he told her he might take a trip too, over to Thalia, while she was gone. He told her he would take the drive in easy stages and be waiting for her in Patagonia when she returned. The night before her departure she almost canceled her plans, but Duane persuaded her to go on. He promised her he'd meet her in Patagonia when she returned.

Reluctantly, she left.

Duane almost didn't make his trip. It was so pleasant to sit on Annie's deck and enjoy the fine sunlight that he almost talked himself out of going home.

Then an emptiness began to assail him—it came whenever Annie was gone. Sometimes, even if she just spent a day shopping in Tucson or Phoenix he felt the emptiness creep in. Annie was due to be away ten days. He didn't want to sit and struggle with the emptiness that long, so he got in his pickup one day and drove along the I-10 to El Paso, where he spent the night in a comfortable downtown hotel. He was still six hundred miles from Thalia but he didn't care. The lights of Juárez, Mexico, glittered in their millions just across the Rio Grande Bridge—he liked to look at the lights and at the people crossing the bridge, but he was not tempted to visit Juárez himself.

The next day he eased on east, through Midland-Odessa, the service towns for the gritty Permian Basin oilfield—one of the great fields of the world. There was a little Petroleum Museum that he had often visited but the emptiness was assailing him—he thought it best to keep on driving. Rather than arrive in Thalia at night he stopped for the second night in Abilene, one hundred miles short of his goal.

Without Annie's bounce and vigor he felt lonely and unmotivated. What had made him think he wanted to go to Thalia anyway? His big house had long since been sold, his old office demolished.

But he had come that far—he got up early and went on.

It was a windy day—a norther was blowing and fine dust swirling in the streets. In his memory of the town where he had spent so much of his life dusty days were the norm, still days the exception.

He thought he would visit the Marlows first—when he knocked on the door Jenny opened it with a crutch. She had a big cast on her right leg but she was cheerful and gave Duane a big hug and a kiss.

"Bad driving finally caught up with me," she said. "A damn flock of wild turkeys flew across the road, causing me to drive straight off into the Little Wichita River—luckily it was nearly dry at the time or I'd have drowned."

"Where's Lester?"

"Gone to Fort Worth to the swap meet," Jenny said. "There's hardly a day passes that Lester can't find some kind of swap meet to go to."

Jenny still had a sparkle in her eyes, and sexy, bony shoulders.

"How long you here for, honey?" she asked.

"I don't know—a few more minutes, I guess," he said. "I just came by to see you and Lester. I can't think of anybody else I even know in this town."

"Are you happily married, Duane?" Jenny asked, looking him in the eye. "I barely met Annie but I liked her."

She smiled.

"I guess that means it's too late for you and me," she said.

It was an old tease they both enjoyed—it had long been too late for the two of them, and yet beneath the tease Duane felt a sadness; perhaps Jenny felt it too.

"Bobby Lee got a penile implant—it's improved his mood no end," Jenny said.

"Bobby Lee got a penile implant?" Duane said, astonished.

"Yep, modern times," Jenny said. "I guess you'll miss him. He's gone to Louisiana with his new sweetie, to a zydeco festival."

"Well, I'll be," Duane said. He gave Jenny Marlow a long hug and a kiss. She had tears in her eyes.

"I've a kind of shadowy feeling that we were more than friends once, maybe back during the boom—you know, when things were a little crazy?"

Jenny shook her head.

"Didn't happen," she said. "You and I were the ones who *weren't* crazy, remember, Duane?"

Duane stopped at the cemetery. He cried at Karla's grave, cried some more at Ruth Popper's.

When he looked back at Thalia all he could see was dust—it had been that way when he had been a teenager, coming in at dawn from a night roughnecking on some oil rig. Thalia was a place where the dust seldom entirely settled.

When he left the cemetery he was crying so hard he scraped the gatepost on the passenger side.

Then, stopping only for gas, he drove back to Arizona, to await the return of his lithe and lovely wife.